MIND BLOWING

St. Leasing – Book 7

L.P. Maxa

ALSO BY L.P. MAXA

RiffRaff Records
Royalty

Legacy

Infamy

Loyalty

Sanctuary

Piracy

Certainty

Inevitably

Finally

The Devil's Share
Play Nice

Play Dirty

Play Fair

Play Softly

Play Hard

Play For Keeps

St. Leasing
Mouth Watering

Breath Taking

Jaw Dropping

Heart Stopping

Soul Crushing

Earth Shattering

Other Novels
Happy Place

Stumbled into Love

Rescued
The Forever Weekend
The Ideal

www.BOROUGHSPUBLISHINGGROUP.com

MIND BLOWING
Copyright © 2022 L.P. Maxa

ISBN: 978-1-957295-20-6

To all the wonderful readers waiting on this one.
Thanks for sticking with me.

ACKNOWLEDGMENTS

This book was a difficult process for me. Not only was it the end of another series, but it was also the end of the first series I ever wrote. My writing career started with St. Leasing. And although it certainly won't stop with St. Leasing, it's bittersweet.

Thank you to everyone who loved these shifters, who wanted more of their story. I think, as with RiffRaff, the younger generation is who I'll miss the most. Riley, Jace, and Jasper.

Thank you to my family for letting me disappear to write. I am surrounded by support, and it means more to me than I could ever articulate.

MIND BLOWING

"The course of true love never did run smooth."

—*William Shakespeare*

Chapter One

Jasper

Jasper loved college. He loved drinking. He loved the freedom from the weight living in Haxton held over his head, especially the darkness he had to immerse himself in when it came to working with his twin. He was happy with his decision to put off school for one semester. He was glad he could be there for Jace and Axie as they tried to save their little slice of the world. Still, the past year had been hard on him and the pack, the constant threat of retaliation from the evil men they were putting behind bars. Jasper was a naturally light person, sarcastic to a fault, and rarely took many things seriously. All those heavy days bummed out his very soul.

Now he was in Greenly, a college freshman, living with his best friend and his best friend's mate. Jasper, Riley, and Blake had a good thing going. They studied together, they ate their meals at the dining room table, and they partied as often as they fucking could. Well. Jasper and Blake partied. Riley spent all his free time on baseball. He was so damn glad Blake was part of their world, otherwise he'd be feeling really fucking lonely. Riley was all business during baseball season. He worked out twice a day, watched every morsel he put into his body, and refused to stay out past nine pm before game days.

Jasper wasn't sure he'd ever had that much discipline for anything in his entire life. He'd played ball back at St. Leasing, but even then he'd partied when he damn well felt like it and didn't give two shits about curfews.

Right now, he was sitting in English Lit, his least favorite class, and the only one he shared with Blake. He was bored out of his mind. The poetry they were going over was difficult to understand. Instead of trying harder to concentrate, he let his gaze wander around the crowded lecture hall. His eyes stopped one row down and to the left. The redhead. He'd noticed her on day one, but she was shy and quiet. She kept her nose in her notes and didn't talk to anyone. She wouldn't be easy, so he'd passed her by for a quicker snack.

They were heading to the end of the semester, and he wouldn't mind something that demanded more effort. Like a final during finals. He snickered at his own joke and Blake jabbed him with her elbow.

He ignored her as he leaned forward. "Psst." He waited semi-patiently as the cute little redhead's gaze cut back to him before quickly looking away again. He tried again, smiling at her dismissal. "Hey." What a nice change of pace. It would make the reward all that much sweeter. "Psssssst." He let his low whisper draw out even longer this time.

She turned slowly to the right, her gaze meeting his, confusion behind those gorgeous green doe eyes. "Yes?"

"I'm Jasper." He held his hand out, pulling his lower lip between his teeth when she simply stared. "And you are?"

Her smile was timid if not cruel, and hot as hell. "Not interested." He snorted, covering the sound with his free hand when her glare narrowed and she shushed him. "You'll get us in trouble."

He groaned, unashamed. "I would fucking love to get into trouble with you, pretty girl." He put out his hand again. "I'm Jasper."

She let out a huff, knocking his attention away with a flick of her wrist. "Callahan, and still not interested."

Callahan. That was a fucking mouthful. It suited her though. Prim, but unique. "Great job on that last midterm, I saw you aced it."

In the short minutes since he'd decided to introduce himself, he'd come up with a plan. It would be foolproof. Nerdy chicks loved to reluctantly tutor the gorgeous players. Every teen movie agreed.

"Yeah, thanks." She wasn't even looking at him now, her attention back to their droning professor.

"I heard you talking the other day. You're in a study club?" She didn't turn around and Blake elbowed him once again. "I was wondering if I could join? I'm nervous about the final and—"

She shook her head. "Sorry, it's full."

"Oh okay. Well maybe you could tutor me instead? I could pay you—"

"I wish I had the time, but um, I don't." The professor dismissed them and she was gone before he could even stand. He watched her hurry away, up the stairs with her books pressed to her chest.

Game on.

***

"Anyone naked?" Jasper knocked, opening Riley and Blake's bedroom door with his hand over his eyes. "Not that I haven't seen it all before." He wasn't an asshole. He gave Riley shit about the one time they'd shared Blake to show him it was nothing. That it didn't mean anything. That he didn't think of her the way he knew Riley did. Blake was his best friend's mate, his whole damn world. And while Jasper loved Blake, cared for her the same as he did his twin's mate, Axie, there were no lingering sexual feelings. Even if he had been inside her tight ass all those months ago.

Riley grabbed a pillow from behind his head and launched it at him. "Hilarious."

"I thought so." Jasper perched on the edge of their bed, high-fiving Blake when she came out of the bathroom dressed in jeans and a cropped t-shirt. "We partying tonight? It's our one free weekend until baseball season is over." Once baseball season ended, it was time for finals.

After that, they'd all head back to Haxton to visit the fam. Put in some face time with all the babies and go on runs with their pack. Jasper hadn't shifted in over a month and his wolf had gone from feeling anxious and caged to forlorn and almost absent.

Riley groaned, looking across the room to his open laptop with the cursor blinking on the blank page. "I have a paper that needs to be turned in by midnight."

"Then it's just me and you, doll face. You game?" Jasper grabbed Blake by the hips and tossed her up the bed toward Riley, ignoring his packmate's growl of protest at his hands on her. "We can get some drinks and you can play wingman. There's this sweet, quiet chick from our English lit class I've been itching to corrupt."

Blake wrinkled her nose. "Callahan? The chick with the freckles?" When Jasper nodded, licking his lips, Blake threw her head back laughing. "You realize you're going after an uninterested redhead, right?"

"So?" Jasper frowned, seemingly confused by her laughter. Callahan was gorgeous, and she refused to give him the time of day. He was primed for the chase. It'd been too long since someone required effort from him. Plus, she acted like he didn't exist, which made him like a dog, more like a wolf, with a bone.

"Your sweet, quiet redheaded best friend got all mated up and won't let you see his dick anymore, so you're replacing him with a female version." Blake giggled, her hand covering her mouth to try to quell her humor. "You see that, right?"

"Why you so obsessed with me, bro?" Riley smirked.

Jasper rolled his eyes and got to his feet. "You two suck." Although he could see the truth of what Blake was saying, as annoying as *that* was. Not about the dick part. He couldn't care less about seeing Riley's schlong. He put his hands on his waist, scowling at a still laughing Blake. "You coming with or not?"

"Oh, I'm not about to miss this." She climbed on Riley's lap, kissing him deeply before hopping up and letting Jasper throw her over his shoulder. "I'll come back home as soon as she turns him down, sourpuss."

Jasper spun around, nearly knocking Blake's head into the doorframe. "I'll drop her ass back home on my way to seal the deal."

"Have fun." Riley got up, sulking his way to his desk and waiting laptop. "Love you."

Both Jasper and Blake yelled, "Love you" back.

***

"I don't even know why we're at this bar, I've never seen Callahan here before." Blake sat up straighter in her seat, peering over the head of their partying peers. "If you really wanted to try your hand, we should've brought flasks to the library."

Jasper snorted into his mug of draft beer. Blake wasn't wrong, Callahan wasn't a barfly. They'd never see her dancing on a table with her hands above her head and her shirt riding up to the edge of her boobs. Although he'd pay good money to see the prim and proper beauty lose control like that. "I have it on good authority it's her roommate's birthday and they're coming by here on their bar crawl."

Blake raised an eyebrow in suspicion. "Callahan is on a bar crawl?" She adjusted her off-the-shoulder pink t-shirt. "Doubtful."

Neither one of them had known Callahan long. She'd been in their English Lit class only this semester. She was easy to read though. She didn't party, she wasn't in a sorority, and she rarely ever spoke to anyone outside of her genius-level study club. Which only had Jasper panting at her heels, wanting to be the one who made her take off that cardigan and show him the bad girl who was no doubt trapped underneath.

"She's DD. It's her gift to her roommate and she's picking them up here."

"How do you even know that?" Blake stole his beer after noticing hers was empty. "Stalk much?"

He raised his hand, signaling their waitress to get them both another round. "I'm not stalking her, jerk face. I fucked her roommate's best friend last week and she was running her mouth nonstop. It was so annoying I had to stick my dick in there to shut her up. But I got all the intel for the bar crawl tonight."

Blake wrinkled her nose, draining the rest of his beer. "I should probably act offended, right? All girl power and angry because you didn't want your hookup to talk? Not to mention, she's one degree removed from the redhead you're chasing."

"You could, but is it really worth it?" They both shook their heads as the waitress marched up to their table. "Can we get another round of the—"

"Really? You aren't even going to acknowledge me?" Their waitress sent Blake a sneer before turning her ire back on Jasper. Her hands were on her hips, her eyes narrowed to tiny brown slits. "Not going to apologize for the other night? Are you serious?"

Blake hid a smile behind her hand as Jasper stared up at the disgruntled dishwater blonde glaring down at them. Jasper cleared his throat, wracking his brain to try to place her. "Uh…." He could recall the girl from last week, but this chick he was having trouble placing. "Um." He cocked his head to the side, letting his eyes travel up and down her body, trying to picture her naked and writhing. "Did we fuck in a bed? Or was it a supply closet? Wait. You're the chick from the bathroom, right?"

She screeched, sounding like a pissed-off crow, before turning on her heel and stomping away.

He grinned across the table, winking at Blake as she shook her head fighting a smile. "You're a disgrace."

He shrugged with a sheepish wince. "I literally don't remember her, and that's bad, even for me." He chuckled, shaking off his brief moment of shame, searching the bar for another waitress he hadn't happened to fuck. "But everyone gets the same shhhhhpiel. One night only. I won't call you. You can't stay the night. Take it or leave it."

Due to his supernatural swagger, most girls weren't so angry when he followed through on his promise of one and done. Here in Greenly though, as Riley had determined last semester, he was more human than shifter. His ability to woo the opposite sex was lying as dormant as his wolf.

"I know. I'm well acquainted with the song and dance you vomit forth. I've heard it, remember?"

Jasper waggled his eyebrows. "Oh, doll face, I remember." She flipped him off and spun out of her seat, heading to the bar to order their drinks straight from the source. He and Riley may've told Blake she only got one night, but she'd never been like the others. Even before Riley knew she was meant to be his forever, his mate, she was different. They were inseparable, their connection formed instantly without them even realizing it. Jasper was lucky he got to still be part of their everyday fairy tale.

The double doors at the front of the bar opened, the air blowing soft red hair all over the place. For a moment in time her auburn locks danced like wildfire. *Callahan.*

His current, well, *goal.* For lack of a better word.

He watched as she made her way through the crowd of wriggling bodies, putting both her delicate hands on the edge of the bar. She stood on her tiptoes, her neck extended, trying to get the attention of the bartender, who was unsuccessfully attempting to flirt with Blake. Jasper got to his feet, making it to both girls in a few long strides. He stood behind them, snapping in the soon-to-be-dead-if-he-didn't-stop-trying-to-get-into-Blake's-very-taken-pants bartender's face. "Hey, this one isn't going to bang you. And this one." He moved his finger from pointing at Blake's head to pointing at Callahan's. "Is too good for you and needs to order a drink."

He barely heard Callahan's soft, "Thank you." Blake handed him his beer and then stayed hidden behind him sipping hers, no doubt eavesdropping. After Callahan had a water placed in front of her, she turned, surveying the rest of the overcrowded bar.

"Are you looking for your roommate? I think she's over by the pool tables in the back." He smiled, trying to appear as nonthreatening as possible. Callahan seemed skittish, like a rabbit ready to bolt at any small disturbance in its atmosphere.

Her stunning green eyes narrowed slightly, her button nose scrunching up. "How do you know who my roommate is? Wait. Never mind. Who are you?"

Jasper ignored the beer that splashed all over his back after Blake spit it out in barely contained laughter. "Jasper." He pointed to himself. "We met the other day, remember? We have English lit together. I asked about your study club." Which was when he'd learned it was full and exclusive, and he wasn't invited. He hadn't cared. He hadn't actually wanted to join. He simply needed a fucking *in* so desperately he was willing to give even library time a try.

"Right." She sipped her water, taking a calculated step away from him. "Okay, still, how do you know who my roommate is? That's, well, unsettling."

"I know your roommate's best friend." Their encounter was *not* going the way he'd hoped it would. Blake was right, he sounded like a stalker to this poor chick. No one wants to nail their stalker, not in real life anyway. "Catherine?"

"Oh. You're *that* Jasper. Delightful." She sent him an altogether withering glance. He knew what that one looked like too. He got them all the time from the females in his pack. "I'll make sure to tell her you said hi." She took another step away.

"Wait."

She glared at him over her shoulder. "Yes?"

"I'm not a dick." Her eyes went wide, as did his. As if they were both shocked at the words tumbling out of his mouth. "I mean, I didn't like screw her over or anything." Was that any better? *Fuck no.*

Callahan nodded slowly, her lips pursed. "Sure. Okay, Jasper. See you around." She disappeared into the crowd before he could utter another ridiculous word.

"That was hilarious, and painful." Blake patted him on the back. "Come on, buddy. Let me buy you a shot." Jasper stuck out his bottom lip, resting his head on her shoulder, more than ready to drink away Callahan's swift rejection.

Two strikes, One more and he was out.

Chapter Two

Jasper

Jasper sat up, his sheets pooling around his waist, his head pounding. Slightly. He was a shifter after all. Hangovers never lasted long thanks to his ability to heal in his sleep. He had to hand it to Blake, that girl knew how to have a hell of a good time. She couldn't drink him under the table, but Jasper was pretty sure if he weren't a shifter with an unnatural metabolism, she'd come damn close.

"My mate is covered in bruises."

Jasper wiped the sleep from his eyes, flopping back down onto his mattress as his best friend stepped into his room with a scowl on his face. Jealousy didn't exist between the three of them, which was why Riley was so okay with Jasper and Blake hanging without him. He didn't love it when Jasper put his hands on her, but there was no anger behind his growls. What did tend to irritate their sensible Riley was them getting too wasted and causing destruction of some form or another.

"Your mate decided to race me home, she tripped on the neighbor's sprinkler." He chuckled. "How in the hell did you land such a crazy chick?" Riley was calm, his personality put everyone around him at ease, like his aura exuded THC. Blake? She was a mini tornado full of energy and blonde curls.

"Opposites attract." Riley sat on the edge of his bed, tossing him a mini bottle of orange juice. "My mate acts a lot like my best friend." He narrowed his eyes. "Apparently, I have a type."

"Well, according to Blake, so do I." Jasper opened the juice, drained it, and then threw the empty toward the trashcan next to his desk. "She's a terrible wingman by the way."

"Blake said, and I quote, 'Callahan handed Jasper his ass and it was epic.'" Riley got up, pulling the covers off Jasper and rolling his eyes at the sight of his bare dick. Jasper refused to sleep in clothes if he could help it. Riley knew what he was most likely getting an eyeful of the moment he whooshed off those warm blankets. "Get dressed. Come with me to the gym."

He frowned, both at the thought of going to the gym so early and Blake's assessment of his interaction with Callahan last night. At least she'd talked to him. That was progress. Sure, she thought he was a fuck-boy dickhead. But she knew who he was. And if Captain Jack Sparrow had taught him anything, that mattered.

Obviously she wasn't the type of chick he usually spent time with. Attention and flirty winks weren't going to get him anywhere with the likes of her. That was okay. He'd step up his game. He'd put in the effort. Something about the ramrod straightness of her spine told him she'd be worth the effort. The repressed ones always were. They tended to let go with a nice side of reckless abandon.

"For fuck's sake, cover your boner and let's go." Riley walked back past his open door, knocking on the wall on his way.

Jasper climbed out of bed, grabbing his cell off the floor where he'd tossed it last night. He had her number. He hadn't wanted to admit that to Blake after she'd already accused him of being a creep. He'd stolen it from her roommate's bff.

He sighed, slipping on some basketball shorts. Texting her was either going to fix the situation or make her get a restraining order.

J: *This is THAT Jasper. I swear I'm not stalking you. I just really need help if I'm going to pass my lit final. I've seen your grades. Your a genius. I was going to ask you last night at the bar, but you blew me off.*

He shoved his cell into his pocket, pulling on a t-shirt on his way down the hall. He wasn't sure if she would even text him back. Riley was waiting at the open front door, throwing him his tennis shoes and ushering him toward his truck. "What's your hurry, bro? I woke up five minutes ago, and I'm hungry as fuck."

"We'll eat after, stop bitching."

Riley climbed behind the wheel, backing out of the driveway as Jasper's phone vibrated in his pocket.

C: *You're*

Jasper knew that would get her brilliant ass. He knew what he was doing, and he knew she wouldn't be able to pass up the chance to correct him and make him look like an idiot. Her opinion of him was low. Not that he could really blame her. He chuckled as he replied.

J: *Damn. You're cold. See? I need your help. Pretty please with ice cream on top? One or two sessions to go over the study guide.*

"Why are you grinning like that? It's weird."

Jasper glanced at Riley before turning back to obsessively watch the three dots appear to show that she was typing again. He hated that he felt a little giddy about it. "I'm trying to get Callahan to agree to tutor me."

"I thought Blake was tutoring you in that class already?"

"She is." Jasper met Riley's eyes. "But you won't let me fuck Blake again, so I need a different tutor." Jasper knew the punch was coming, so he braced for it. The bruise it was going to leave on his arm would match the one on the other side from the last time he'd made an inappropriate mate joke.

C: *Two sessions, one hour each, at the library.*

Hmmm. The library. It was going to be hard to get her to agree to fooling around there, but not impossible. He'd done more with less.

J: *One at the library, one at my house? Please. Let me repay you with some DoorDash.*

C: *No.*

J: *Look. You think I'm an asshole, and maybe I deserve that. But I'm not all bad. I live with Blake and my best friend. They'll be*

there, and I'm sure Blake would love to do an extra study session before the final, she's in our class too.

Jasper knew Blake would be pissed he was using her to lure Callahan to the house, but desperate times called for desperate measures. He'd buy Blake a present. Maybe a bottle of tequila? Or a butt plug. Once you had two shifters double team you, normal sex had to be boring AF.

C: Fine. One session at the library, one at your house WITH Blake there the whole time. You buy dinner, and you bring me coffee to the library sesh.

"Got her, bro." Jasper did a little happy dance in his seat.

J: Deal.

Riley sighed, shaking his head slowly as he pulled into the gym parking lot. "I'm torn between high-fiving you or telling you that your antics are reprehensible."

Jasper shrugged, opening his door and hopping out. "Well, we both know Blake will high-five me, so if it'll make you feel better, you can lecture me while we warm up on the treadmill." Pointedly, he put in his ear pods, letting his best friend know his talking would fall on deaf ears. "While you're in lecture mode, how would you feel about me buying your mate a butt plug as an ask-for-forgiveness-not-permission gift?"

This time bracing for the punch didn't help. Riley drew down the back of his hand and hit Jasper in the balls.

Hard.

Chapter Three

Jasper

Jasper was at the library for the first time all semester. He wasn't a dumbass and he was passing most of his classes with a B-ish. However, English was never his strong suit. He actually needed tutoring, but Blake had gotten his average up from a D to a C, and he was more than okay with a passing grade.

What he wasn't okay with was not attempting to get with Callahan. He knew he sounded gross, like a fuck-boy of epic proportions. This was how he looked at it though: his sexcapades had a deadline. One day, he'd meet his girl and they'd settle down and then he'd fuck only her for the rest of time. He was like a dying man at a buffet. He had to sample it all before he could only eat steak for the rest of his life. Shifters weren't like humans. He'd never cheat on his mate, he'd never want anyone else, sexually or otherwise. So, while he could, he was going to live it the fuck up.

Enter classy, repressed little Callahan.

"You're early." She came in, all business, set down a laptop, a tablet, and two spiral notebooks. "I was sure you would get lost trying to find the library."

Jasper smiled, not at all put off by her bristling attitude. "Blake drew me a map." He scooted her coffee cup closer to her, wanting her to see he hadn't forgotten. She hadn't told him what kind, so he'd gone with a latte as a safe bet.

"Blake. That was the blonde you were with at the bar?"

Jasper bit his lips together to keep his growing grin in check. Callahan had noticed he was out with another girl even when she was handing him his ass and attempting to appear unaffected? Noted.

"Blake is my best friend's girlfriend." He cleared his throat and pulled out his notes, the ones he'd copied from said blonde.

"Why isn't she tutoring you then?" Callahan lined up three sharpened pencils in a neat row, then tucked her legs underneath her. She was so tiny she could easily sit in a comfy ball on the narrow library chair. His eyes moved down her body, wanting nothing more than to pluck her from her position and have her sit somewhere else.

His face.

Jasper cleared that lovely mental image from his mind, focusing on simply getting Callahan to like him. They could work on him eating her like dessert later. "She was, but now she's cramming for some chemistry test that has her all worried." That wasn't a total lie. Blake was studying around the clock for her chem final. It was her self-proclaimed hardest class. If he'd asked her for help though, she would've made time for him.

"I assume you have your study guide filled out already?" By the tone of her question, she presumed he'd shown up without the study guide complete, and she'd walk. Good thing he'd copied that off Blake too.

"Yep." He opened the Word file on his laptop, a fully complete and correct study guide. "I have this pretty much memorized. But the syllabus said we'll need to do a mini essay on one of the poems we went over. Poetry isn't my jam." Also not a lie. *At all.* He hated poetry, and he really needed some help there.

See? He wasn't a complete douche.

He was simply an opportunist.

Callahan pushed a tablet to him. "The poems we went over this semester are saved here, we can pick one and dissect it. We shouldn't pick the same one though, because our points would be too similar."

"Okay, great, thank you. I really appreciate your help." He sent her his most genuine smile. He did appreciate her help, but he also appreciated that she smelled like caramel apples, and her white t-shirt let him get a peek at her cleavage.

"I'm doing *The Bee Keeper's Daughter*, so how about *Sonnet 129* by Shakespeare?" She propped up her tablet, lightly tapping the screen until the poem was in front of them. "This one is shorter, and it seems right up your alley."

"Cool." His eyes narrowed as he re-read one of the poems they'd gone over at the beginning of the semester. He'd done terrible on that test. That was where his D average came from. "But why is this one *up my alley*?" He refrained from telling her he wanted to be up *her* alley—he doubted she would've valued the joke.

"Really? Did you read the poem?"

He could feel her gaze cut to his, but he was still trying to get through old William's confusing-as-fuck way of writing. He sighed, coming to the last line: *To shun the heaven that leads men to this hell.* "Yes, I read the poem more times than I care to admit. Doesn't mean I understood it. I already told you, poetry is hard for me." He let humility leak into his tone. None of it was for show, and his honesty seemed to soften her a bit.

Her shoulders dropped slightly from their seemingly permanent place by her ears. "I'm sorry. I'm being rude. Poetry is hard for a lot of people." She took a deep breath, almost as if she were fortifying herself with patience. "This sonnet is about lust, which tracks because all the poems our professor picked this semester dealt with sex in one way or another."

His eyes went wide. "Huh. You'd think I would've done better on material all about sex and lust." That showed how little the fancy and veiled words registered in his brain. Now he was glad he'd asked for Callahan's help, for real this time.

She licked her lips, pointing back to the screen and choosing not to comment on his self-deprecation. "This one in particular discussed lust in three parts. Lust before it's acted on, the act itself, and then the remnants left after two people come together." He wanted them to *come* together. He barely contained his snort of laughter. These hilarious gems he was keeping to himself were killing him. "When you write your essay, I'd do three or four sentences on each section."

He leaned closer, his face next to hers as she used a stylist to draw lines throughout the sonnet, showing him which parts belonged together. "Lust as an idea, as the buildup, right?" He pointed to the first few lines: *The expense of spirit in a waste of shame is lust in action.* He was speaking softly, not out of respect for the other people studying, but to see if he could get goose bumps to break out on Callahan's arms. "If you ask me, lust is never a waste."

Her breath hitched, slightly. If he wasn't paying such rapt attention, he'd have missed it. "Wait 'til the end of your essay to state any personal opinions. Our professor will want to know you fully grasp the meaning of the poem first."

He nodded and continued: *Had, having, and in quest to have, extreme; a bliss in proof...*" He took her hand in his, using her stylist to underline that line. "Bliss in proof. Sex. Fulfilling the lust."

Her audible swallow made his dick twitch in his joggers. He bit his lips together to keep from smiling. This little tutoring session was going better than he could've ever expected. If he'd have known they'd be seated close, dissecting an old-school porn poem, he'd have begged her to help him weeks ago.

"Yes." She cleared her throat, sitting back, making him miss her scent and her warmth. "And then it's over and he describes it as a woe, a dream, a hell." He chuckled, rubbing his thumb along his lower lip, intentionally drawing her attention to his mouth. Her beautiful evergreen eyes narrowed slightly. "Shakespeare says lust is mad, in any form. Before, during, and after. That's what the poem speaks to, and that's what the body of your essay needs to do."

"Lust is madness, there's no denying that." He was whispering, his gaze holding hers. "But I'd happily go crazy before ever giving it up." Ah, there were those gorgeous goose bumps he'd been working for. He reached a finger out, trailing it lightly down her arm.

She jerked away from his attention, quickly closing out the tablet and gathering her stuff against her chest. "Like I said, if you have a differing opinion, you can add it in the end."

"You leaving? Our hour isn't up." He leaned back in his seat, crossing his arms, marveling at the blush creeping across Callahan's cheeks.

"Write a rough draft of your essay, I'll go over it the next time we meet and let you know if you need to do anything differently for the final." She refused to look at him, choosing to focus on packing up, pushing her chair neatly back under the table. "I'll text you when I'm free again. Thanks for the coffee." She turned on her heel, hurrying out of the library like someone was chasing her.

He couldn't contain his smile.

Chapter Four

Jasper

A whole day passed before Callahan texted him to say she could meet him the next night. He had itched to reach out first, to make her speak to him. Instead, he'd let Riley drag him to the gym twice as a distraction. He knew he was closer to having her, to tasting that sweet apple scent. He'd affected her at the library, and she'd run because he'd turned her on.

He'd promised her dinner, so he'd ordered enough Chinese food to feed his entire pack. And he'd gotten down on his knees and begged Blake and Riley to join them downstairs. As expected, Blake was not pumped to be used in his pursuit of the beautiful redhead. Also as expected, his gift had smoothed things over. He'd gone for the tequila since even mentioning the butt plug had gotten him knocked in the nuts.

"Are you in love with this chick?" Blake was shoveling lo mein into her mouth with the finesse of a drunk sumo wrestler. "This is more effort than I've ever seen you make for anything or anybody."

He had their food neatly arranged on the coffee table, he'd cleaned both the downstairs bathroom and his own. In case he actually got her up to his room tonight. He had his essay typed and printed for her to look over. He'd even went out and bought her a red pen so she could mark it all to hell if she needed to.

"No, I'm not in love. I'm in lust." He tapped the paper he'd sat on the coffee table beside the broccoli and beef. "Shakespeare says it makes one a little bit mad." He grinned, happy with himself for not only understanding the poem, but using it to relate to real life, like a true scholar.

"Well, mad I'll give you." Riley plopped down on the couch, his gray sweats making Jasper wrinkle his nose.

"Go change, quick, before she gets here."

Riley glanced down at his casual outfit. "Why the hell do I need to change? We're at home, eating Chinese food on the couch. *My* finals are done, and in about thirty minutes I'm going to pull my mate upstairs and hold my hand over her mouth while I make her come on repeat."

Blake licked her lips and perched on Riley's lap, making Jasper roll his eyes in annoyance. "While I truly appreciate you muffling the overly loud sound of Blake's orgasms while we have company, I need you to change anyway. You're wearing sweatpants that make the outline of your dick clearly visible."

"So are you." Riley gestured to Jasper's own barely hidden bulge.

Jasper tugged up Blake, then hauled Riley to his feet as well. "Well, yeah. But I want Callahan to notice *my* dick, not yours." Jasper put his palms together, pleading. "If you go change, I swear I won't mention that one time we both fucked Blake until fall semester starts."

His best friend's eyes narrowed in challenge. "'Til spring semester."

"Uh, how about you never mention it again, ever?" Blake stated.

Both shifters ignored her. Riley and Jasper knew he wouldn't be able to go the rest of time without making jokes about their one and only threesome. There was no reason to set himself up for failure.

"Deal. Spring semester." He pointed to the second floor. "Now change. She should be here any minute."

Riley stomped up the stairs, irritated, but doing what Jasper wanted nonetheless. Blake sat, going back to her box of greasy noodles. "You're acting like a real loon, you know that, right? You could walk down sorority row and end up in an orgy if you so pleased, so what gives with this girl?"

"She doesn't want me." He peered down at the pretty girl who stole his best friend's heart and soul. "I'm a wolf. The chase is making me fucking giddy."

"That sounds like you're on your way to a felony."

He scoffed. "I'd never hurt her, or anyone for that matter." Although that wasn't entirely true, was it? He'd almost hurt Madden, and then Blake. He'd wanted Axie, and if Riley hadn't pulled him away, he'd have bitten her. He hated his wolf for reacting so strongly to the unfulfilled mating call of a woman's body. If he could change anything about himself, that would be it. "I mean, I uh, it's not like that with her. I—"

"Stop." Blake reached up, taking his hand in hers. "You aren't a criminal, and I know you would never intentionally harm anyone like that. Even on your most wolfish days, you've never crossed that line. I was joking. I wasn't trying to make you feel bad. I love you. You know that."

"I love you too."

His grip tightened in hers as Riley came bounding down the stairs. "Quit touching my mate." He popped him on the back of the head before joining them on the couch in a pair of basketball shorts.

Chapter Five

Callahan

Blake and her boyfriend went upstairs almost an hour ago, and yet she was still seated on the couch next to the incorrigible Jasper. She should've left the moment they were alone together. Their time in the library made her admit he was a real person with feelings and thoughts. Then he'd gone and given her chills with his softly spoken words about lust and Shakespeare. She could count on one hand the number of times she'd experienced lust in her entire life. *Jasper.* He'd made her want him, and for a small moment in time she'd imagined climbing into his lap and begging him to keep whispering *Sonnet 129* in her ear.

She gave herself a mental head shake, choosing to concentrate on the real reason she was here in his house, surrounded by his spicey scent and greasy Chinese food. "Your essay is really good." She handed it back to him, with only a few notes and corrections made in red ink. "I have no doubt you'll pass the final tomorrow."

"Really?" His grin grew as she nodded in response. "Will you come over to celebrate after? We could have a drink, maybe go out with Blake and Riley for a couple hours?"

She wanted to say yes, which was exactly why she wouldn't. "I can't." She stood, a small frown on her face, like she was sorry she'd turned him down. She wasn't sorry though. She was full of self-preservation and inhibitions. The way she'd been so carefully raised to be. "I have other plans." Plans that included packing to move home for the summer before falling asleep alone in her dorm room, reading a romance novel, and eating a sleeve of Girl Scout cookies.

"Oh, okay." His disappointment was clear, his pretty eyes losing some of their light. Jasper tended to deflate a bit every time she told him no. She chose not to dwell on why it always made her take pause and consider changing her mind. "I guess I'll see you tomorrow in class?"

"Yeah, see you tomorrow." She picked up her bag, shoving her cell into the front pocket. "Thanks for dinner." She shut the front door before she could even hear his response.

She put all thoughts of Jasper out of her mind for as long as it took for her to climb into bed with her Kindle and her cookies. She sighed, glancing around her lonely half-packed dorm room. Her roommate was always out having fun and meeting up with friends. At first she used to invite Callahan along. But after so many times of Callahan turning her down, she'd stopped. She'd been away at college for two semesters and she could count the number of good times she'd had on one hand. How sad was that? Sure she had a sparkling GPA, and an empty TBR list. But what was it worth?

She'd enjoyed Jasper's company, and he'd turned out to have some actual humility and substance. She wanted to see him again, so why push that desire away? Who knew when she'd feel it again? She was going home for the summer, which meant she'd be boring and repressed, and stuck with her family. Might as well experience a small piece of college life while she had the chance. She doubted she'd even see Jasper again next semester.

She plucked her phone off the charger, pulling up his name.

C: My plans changed. You still want to meet up tomorrow after the final?

J: Yes

His response came immediately and she wondered if his phone had been open already.

J: Thanks again for helping me. This is the most confident I've felt going into a test. Ever.

She enjoyed tutoring people, and she'd felt incredibly guilty when she'd turned him down the first time he'd asked her about the study club. She'd seen him in class flirting with girls and laughing with Blake. It didn't seem like he took himself or the class seriously.

Why would she want to help someone who wasn't helping themselves? Not to mention he had a reputation around campus. One that promised he was after one thing and one thing only, and once he got it you'd never hear from him again.

Apparently, he was worth the good time because girls flocked to him like flies to honey. That wasn't who she was. Definitely not who she ever wanted to be. Another notch on some hot guy's bedpost? No thanks. She couldn't deny her attraction to him though. He was gorgeous. But it'd been his eagerness to grasp the material that made her take notice.

And the way his whispered recitation of Shakespeare felt against her skin.

C: You're welcome. And it's a group thing, right? Blake and Riley will be there?

J: Yeah. Don't worry Callie, your virtue will be safe and sound.

She frowned, re-reading his words more than once.

C: I'm not worried about my virtue.

She had complete control over herself and her actions. Sure, Jasper was handsome and charismatic with a long list of qualities that seemed to make the girls on campus fall all over themselves for a chance to be with him. Her convictions were stronger than his magnetism.

J: Aren't you tho? You refuse to be alone with me.

This was the side of Jasper she wasn't a fan of. The side that said he knew his effect on most women and he found it adorable.

C: I refuse to be alone with you because I don't want that overinflated head of yours getting the wrong idea. This isn't a date. I won't be spending the night in your bed, and I don't want you thinking otherwise.

There. The truth all laid out. He could rescind his invitation to go out if he wanted to, but she refused to play his games. She wasn't a conquest. She thought more highly of herself than that. He turned her on, he did. He made her yearn for his touch, that was true. Every desire wasn't meant to be acted on though.

J: Damn Callie baby, you go right for the throat, huh? I can respect that. This is definitely not a date (I don't date), and I know you won't be spending the night (no one does). I'll be on my best behavior, and I give Riley and Blake permission to kick my ass if you ask them to.

Callie baby. She didn't love it. She refused to admit that to him though. She figured he'd keep using the nickname to get a rise out of her. Jasper was like a seven-year-old boy on the playground, getting girls' attention by jokes and veiled flirtation.

C: See you tomorrow. Good luck on your test.

J: You too.

She clicked off her bedside lamp, snuggling under the covers with only the light of her Kindle for company.

She knew what she was doing, she was a smart girl. She could go out and have some fun without letting things get out of hand. Her parents raised her to be responsible, sensible, and virtuous.

In short, they raised her to be everything that Jasper was not.

Chapter Six

Jasper

Jasper had aced the test. No doubt in his mind. He actually enjoyed taking it too. Writing his opinion on the sonnet was fun. Once he understood what the flowery words meant, he found he had a lot of thoughts he wanted to share.

He hit submit on his tablet, standing and stretching his tight muscles and looking around for Blake and Callahan. They were both gone, so he headed up the stairs and out of the large lecture hall. Riley was coming to meet them and then the four of them were going out for drinks. That's what Callahan agreed to, so that was the game plan.

He'd basically had to beg Blake to be his buffer again. She demanded he take her house chores for two weeks and do two loads of her laundry. Joke was on her. He sent his laundry out.

Riley, Blake, and Callahan were standing near the front entrance waiting for him. "Well?" Callahan smiled expectantly when she saw him, which made his heart sing, just a bit.

"Aced it." He held his hand up, high-fiving her. "Couldn't have done it without you." He threaded their fingers together and used his grip to pull her in for a quick, non-threatening hug. "Thanks again."

She nodded, her eyes on the ground as she stepped away from him. "You're welcome."

He opened the door, holding it so his friends could all file out. "Where to, Callie? Any requests?" She shook her head, her lips pressed between her teeth. He wondered what it would take for such a stunning girl to loosen up and have some fun. "Okay, let's hit that bar we saw you at the other night. It'll be empty and we can pick all the music on that old-school jukebox."

They walked together toward the parking lot. Earlier, Riley had dropped Blake and him off for their test and had gotten in a workout while he waited. Riley was responsible, for the most part. But he sure as hell knew how to have a good time when it was warranted. "I'll drive us there, and we can always call a ride if we end up drinking the rest of the day way." He winked at his mate, pulling her close for a kiss that was inappropriate if not their usual. "I'm done letting my girl and my best friend have all the fun around here."

"Aw, sourpuss, you can join our party anytime you want." She ruffled his hair as he opened her car door.

Riley smiled as he buckled her in, being an overprotective shifter in front of a very human Callahan. "The ringleader has to control the dancing clowns, not get drunk with them."

Jasper held Callie's door, wanting to make the effort and a good impression. "Ignore Riley, he's just bitter that Blake loves him only slightly more than she loves me."

Callahan smiled at his comment and Riley growled low in his throat as Blake groaned. "Don't make him all cranky before he's even started to have fun, jerk-face."

Jasper held his hands up in surrender. "I already promised Callie, I'll be on my very best behavior."

Blake barked out a laugh. "That'll be the day."

Callahan was quiet, sitting with her small hands in her lap as she watched campus give way to the small downtown area of Greenly. He knew she was uncomfortable. He could feel the tension coming off her. His wolf may be taking the world's longest nap, but even a human could pick up on the vibes she was putting out.

He reached over, tapping her thigh and appreciating the short sundress she was rocking. "I'm glad you decided to come with us." She nodded, lips in a tight smile. Everything about her was coiled to snap, and he was beyond fucking hopeful that he'd be the one who was around when it happened.

***

Turned out, two beers were the key to unlocking Callahan's personality. She and Blake were dancing on the empty floor to old-school Taylor Swift. He'd handed them a stack of dollar bills about five minutes ago and now he was sure he, Riley, and the other three random dudes in the bar were about to listen to a full hour of girl anthems.

"Who knew she could laugh?" Riley nudged him with his elbow as Blake spun a giggling Callie around. "She's even prettier when she lets go a bit."

"Get your eyes off my hot tutor or I'll tell Blake and watch as she removes your testicles with a spoon." Jasper smiled against his beer bottle, happily watching the two beauties have a good time and dance like, literally, no one was watching. "But, yeah, I agree."

"Why this girl, man?" Riley pointed at her. "Why work so hard when you could walk into any lecture hall and find a sure thing? Is there something else going on here?"

"If you're asking if my wolf wants to claim her sweet little soul for eternity, the answer is no." Jasper's wolf didn't seem to give two shits about the girl he was lusting after. "I think it all stems from that age-old she-doesn't-want-me-so-I-have-to-have-her deal. It's a disgrace, I know, I don't need the lecture."

"No lecture." Riley held his hands up. "I only want to make sure you're seeing this clearly, that you know what you're doing. She's innocent, really fucking innocent. Messing with her could have some repercussions."

"Clingy?" He'd already thought of that. "She leaves in like a week and a half once the dorms close. I won't even have a chance to see her again for three full months. That's plenty of time and space to let any delusional hearts in her eyes die out." He didn't want to hurt her, that wasn't part of his plan. He'd never intentionally hurt anyone. "She'll get the same talk they all get: one hell of a good time and nothing more. I don't lie." And with few exceptions here and there, most chicks were fine with the bare minimum he had to offer.

"Come dance with me, sourpuss." Blake grabbed Riley's hand, dragging him out onto the dance floor and shooting Jasper a wink and a nod toward a now solo Callahan.

Blake wasn't the worst wingman after all.

Jasper downed his beer, placing it on the bar behind him before sauntering out into the open space they'd created. He held out his hand. "What do you say, Callie baby?" She licked her bottom lip, indecision in her gaze for all of two seconds before she let him pull her into his body.

The song switched over to something a little less pop and more vintage soul. "Sandman" by BRONCHO. He held Callie close, his hand on her lower back, his knee between her pretty little thighs. Dancing he could do.

They moved around the floor for three more songs, her body becoming more pliant with every note. Her fingers moved into the hair on the back of his head, twisting and playing in a way that was driving him wild.

"Careful, Callie, I could get used to your touch." He spoke against her ear, pleased she pulled him closer instead of pushing him away like she'd been doing for the past week.

Chapter Seven

Callahan

Callahan was sure she'd never had as much fun as she was having in that moment. Blake was as kind and welcoming as Riley was calm and reassuring. Jasper? Jasper was, surprisingly, the best part. He danced like it was as natural as walking. He never pointed out when she missed a step or moved with inexperience. He held her close, making her smile and laugh with every dip and spin. His legs tangling with hers was what she assumed sin was born from. She wanted his touch, she wanted to touch him in return. She wanted to go back in time and do *more* of this. She wanted a redo of her freshman year. Filling it with friends and silly nights of dancing in empty gritty bars instead of nonstop studying and seclusion.

She was drunk on fun, and only fun. She'd had two beers, and that was hours ago. The bar was starting to fill with coeds, done with finals for the day and looking to unwind the way they had. The four of them were sitting at a small round table, laughing at one story after another of Blake living with two guys for the first time.

"Your parents didn't mind you moving in with your boyfriend?" Callahan's parents wouldn't have even entertained the thought. It was simply something that wouldn't have been allowed.

Riley put his arm around Blake, kissing her temple. "I went to meet them, of course, and I asked their permission. I told them that I was in love with their daughter, that I planned to keep loving her for the rest of time, and I asked if she could live with me. I told her dad I wanted to know that she was safe, always. Her mom swooned and they said yes."

"My mom did not swoon." Blake rolled her eyes, gently shoving his face away. "And my dad threatened to murder you if you broke my heart or got me pregnant."

"Either way, we've been living together ever since." Riley winked.

Jasper had his forearm resting on the back of Callahan's chair, and she hated how much she liked it. Despite herself, she was beginning to enjoy his attention and all the things she'd promised before agreeing to hang out with him. "I thought living with a girl would be nice, that she'd keep things neat and clean. Nope. Blake is the actual messiest person I've ever met."

She scoffed. "I am not."

He pulled Callahan closer, speaking into her ear like he was telling a secret. "She is."

She'd never craved attention like that. Every time he touched her, spoke only to her, butterflies took flight in the pit of her stomach.

"This bar is getting too crowded, let's pick up some food and eat at the house." Riley stretched his arms over his head, and then gathered Blake into his lap. "Too many dudes looking at my girl, it's making me twitchy under my skin."

"Yeah, I should head home, I have another final the day after tomorrow." It was what she *should* do. That was the responsible move, the move she would normally make. She found herself disappointed though, bummed at the thought of leaving the three of them and going back to her empty dorm room and bland food from the dining hall.

Jasper stood, helping her to her feet. "You sure? You could eat with us and then I could take you home after."

He'd given her an out, he'd provided her with exactly what she wanted. A way to drag out the night, a way to keep this giddy feeling inside her from disappearing. Her brain was at war: what she should do and what she wanted to do. "Well, yeah, okay. That sounds good."

The truth was, she wasn't ready to say good-bye. She'd wished on the dance floor for a redo, to have more fun.

There was no harm in her indulging herself now.

She would be home and back to boring and sensible in no time anyway.

***

Dinner was takeout, again. Riley said he liked to cook, but he'd had too much beer to care. They piled on the couch and ate every last morsel of the Greek food they'd picked up on their ride home. An old movie was on TV, but no one was paying much attention to it.

Riley dragged Blake to her feet, then playfully threw her over his shoulder. "Callahan, it was nice to see you again." He winked at her, gesturing his head to the flat-screen mounted on the wall. "Turn up the volume." Blake giggled and waved good-bye as he carted her up the stairs.

Callahan wiped her hands, gathering the empty cartons.

"Don't worry about that, you're our guest. You don't need to clean." Jasper took the containers from her, carrying them into the kitchen before dumping them in the trash. "You want to watch another movie?"

"I should go." She licked her lips, resigned to the fact that she prolonged her one night of fun for as long as possible. The movie was over, dinner was done, Blake and Jasper were in bed, and it was getting late.

"There's a big difference between *should go* and wanting to leave." He came back into the room, his eyes alight with a sense of mischief she'd come to recognize. "Which one is it, Callie?" She stayed rooted in place, unable to move or look away. She was trapped by him, by the feelings he stirred inside. She never met anyone like him. "Because I want you to stay with me."

"I thought you didn't do sleepovers." It was the first thing she could think to say.

He chuckled, taking a step closer to her. "You won't be getting much sleep, baby."

He was standing in front of her, calling her baby and asking her to stay the night. She'd never been propositioned like this before. He was forward and bold, everything she wasn't. Everything she'd been raised to fear and avoid. He spoke without a filter, and he wasn't ashamed of how he was feeling.

She wished she was a little more like him. Maybe she was drunk on the fun and the freedom from their day together. Maybe she was simply tired of being so lonely and reserved. Either way, she wanted this. She wanted one wild experience, one crazy story from college. And Jasper, well, he really was the perfect candidate, wasn't he?

"Okay." She dropped her shoulders, her gaze darting from him to the top of the stairs where she assumed his room was located. "Okay, I'll stay."

She smiled at the surprise in his eyes before he worked to disguise it. He thought she'd turn him down again. He thought he'd be driving her home.

Yeah well, so did she.

Here they were though, negotiating a night together.

"If this, if *I'm*, what you want, then I will give to you freely. All fucking night. But I won't lie to you. I won't pretend hearts and flowers are waiting for you at the end of this. When you leave here, friends are all we'll ever be. Do you understand?"

"Yes." It was the perfect setup. She wasn't in love, and he didn't seem capable of the emotion.

He stepped forward, grabbing her hand and pulling her into his arms. He kissed her, and everything tilted. She was dizzy with it. She'd never been kissed so thoroughly in her life. Not that she had many kisses to compare it to.

His lips parted, moving hers as well, opening her to him. He kissed her deeper, towering over her and commanding her compliance. He lifted her, carrying her up the stairs without taking his lips off hers. Before she knew it, she was on his bed, his body dwarfing hers.

He pulled back, smiling down at her. "You sure this is what you want? I—"

"I'm not some stupid virgin, Jasper. Don't treat me like one." She was irritated he wasn't ravaging her. From the moment he kissed her, she hadn't wanted him to ever stop. She didn't want to talk this out or reassure him. She wanted to get lost in their one night together.

"Huh, really?" He pursed his lips. "I would've bet money I was about to be your first." She rolled her eyes. Arrogant silly boy. "Tell me about him."

"Who?"

"The guy I plan to erase from your memory." Her core ached at his softly spoken words. She wasn't sure she'd ever get used to the things he said so easily. Although one night only meant she'd never have to.

She shook her head, tightening her thighs around his hips. She didn't want to talk about her past. She didn't want to sober from his kisses.

"Tell me, baby, I want to know."

Baby. She wished he'd stop calling her that. It sounded too sweet coming from his lips. A sweet, sweet little lie.

"There isn't much to tell." She tugged at his hair, because she could. "We were seventeen, at church camp."

He chuckled, his gaze playful. "Cliché."

"Says the college fuck-boy."

"Touché." He dipped down, nipping at the column of her throat, making her core clench. "Also the first time I've heard a cuss word leave those adorable lips. Not going to lie, it's hot." He kissed his way across her collarbone, from shoulder to shoulder. "Tell me one more time, is this what you really want?"

She arched her back as his mouth moved to her breasts. "Yes."

It was exactly what she wanted. Exactly what she needed.

One fun night.

One night to be nothing more than a college freshman, living life out loud.

Chapter Eight

Jasper

Now that Jasper had her here, underneath him, he was more hesitant than he'd ever been before. He needed to take his time. He didn't want to upset her. She wasn't like the girls he typically hooked up with. He couldn't pump into her without his body ever touching the mattress and send her on her merry little way. She was shy, although she'd surprised him when she boldly said she wanted to stay.

He moved her dress up her body, placing soft kisses along her stomach, her ribs, while his fingers worked their way along her thighs to pull off her panties. She was squirming under his touch, her fingers in his hair.

He put his palms on her knees, pushing them back until he could see all of her. He hummed in appreciation, as she seemed to tense against his touch. Her legs tried to close, like she was embarrassed by being completely bare for him. He shook his head, a smirk on his lips. "You're beautiful, I want to see you. I want to taste you. Every fucking inch." He swooped in to taste her. She was sweet, so damn responsive to his every touch.

He kissed his way to her core, licking and sucking until she was gasping his name. He slid two fingers inside her pussy, obsessed with the sounds she was making. He moved them in and out of her tight body, only stopping when her thighs were shaking from her first orgasm. He would bet money the kid at church camp hadn't touched her like this. Hadn't played her body until she was whimpering incoherently.

Satisfied she would be more than ready, he kneeled over her, pulling off his shirt. He took notice as she began to sober again, covering her breasts with one arm, squeezing her knees shut on either side of him.

"None of that now." He shook his head. "Didn't we just talk about this? You're perfect." She dropped her arm, a timid grin on her face. "I love the way you come undone."

He kissed her senseless, wanting her need for him grow again, to be insatiable, like his was for her. Her fingers fumbled with his belt and he couldn't help but laugh quietly at how inexperienced she was.

He fucking adored it. She was letting go for him, *with* him. He felt honored.

He pushed his briefs down, reaching over her head into his bedside drawer. He grabbed a handful of condoms, putting one on and laying the rest beside her. He palmed her thigh, hiking it up his hip and positioning himself at her center. He glanced up at her, making sure she was still there, still with him. Still wanted him. He entered her slowly, inch by inch, his head falling back at how fucking amazing she felt.

He moved slowly at first, letting her get used to the stretch of having someone inside her. Three years was a long time to go in between partners, and if he broke her on round one, their night would end quicker than he wanted. He took his time, watching for each and every tell. He took notice of what she liked, what made her hiss, and what made her stop breathing.

Once she was writhing underneath him, begging for more, he let go. He held her hips off the bed with his grip on her creamy thigh, angling deeper. He thrust into her over and over, her cries growing louder each time he bottomed out inside her.

She felt so damn good as she came, holding him hostage until he tumbled over the edge with her.

***

Jasper was awake, staring at the ceiling, listening to Callie's soft breathing next to him. Three times, he'd made her come three times, then she'd passed out. He couldn't blame her, and to be honest, he felt super fucking smug about it. He rolled onto his side, taking in her peaceful expression. She was completely relaxed, unaware of how much he wanted her again. He watched her for a few moments, debating whether he should wake her. He didn't do sleepovers in the first place, so on principle alone... He trailed his finger down the column of her slender throat, hooking it into his sheets and pulling them down her body until she was exposed to him once more.

She was beautiful, her skin flawless and soft. No piercings, no tattoos. Nothing branding her but him.

She stirred, her eyes opening, her gaze on his. "What's wrong?"

He shook his head, his signature smirk in place. "No sleeping, remember?"

She turned to look at his clock; it was old-school with large red digital numbers. "That's some alarm clock."

He could hear the humor in her tone. "That alarm clock is relentless. It's too old to care about snooze, and screams at me until I get my lazy butt out of bed." He reached for another condom, gesturing with his chin. "Roll over, baby." Her breath seemed to catch in her throat, her eyes going impossibly wide at his words, or what they suggested. Either way it didn't matter. "Trust me."

She had no reason to. Still, she turned over on her stomach as he threw all the blankets off his bed and onto the floor. He grabbed her hips, lifting her until she was on all fours. She glanced behind her, a frown on her pretty face. He leaned down, capturing her lips, kissing her until she was arching her back and searching for a release. She may be nervous, but her body knew exactly what he promised.

He pulled back, fisting her long hair as he slid inside her once more. He took his time, making sure not to hurt, worried that she was sore from their first couple of rounds. He moved in and out of her pussy, burying himself to the hilt each time, loving the whimpers she made.

No one had ever sounded as sexy as Callie. It was like each noise she made was equal parts shock and ecstasy. She rested forehead on his mattress, changing the angle and inadvertently letting him invade deeper. She gasped. He chuckled.

"You like that, see? I told you to trust me." He popped her ass, enjoying the red hue that blushed across her skin. She began to meet him, every thrust, chasing her release. "That's it, good girl." He slammed into her, relentlessly, until her cries reached a peak and her pussy contracted around him. He moved through her orgasm, drawing it out as he came.

She collapsed onto her stomach as he disposed of the condom. "You need another nap, baby?"

"Nap? No. I need real sleep. I think I'm tapped out." She was curled in a ball. The window was open, and the cooler night breeze was giving her chills without the blankets. He picked them up, dragging them over her.

He lay beside her, pushing her long tangle of hair off her face. If she was done, then she should leave. Though he couldn't seem to say the words out loud. The thought of kicking her out of his bed, his house, it felt cruel.

He peeked at the clock on the other side of her. There were only a few hours until morning. A few hours' sleep was nothing more than a nap anyway. He pulled her closer, breathing in her sweet scent as he began to doze off.

Chapter Nine

Jasper

Jasper woke up with a small, freckled nose breathing against his neck. He'd allowed Callahan to stay the night, and that wasn't his usual way of ending his extracurricular activities. If he was feeling nice, he'd call them a car service. Sleepovers were not part of the deal. Callahan had been different through. Different in the way he hadn't been able to get enough of her soft cries and her nails raking down his back. He'd fucked her over and over until they'd had no choice but to simply pass out. He told her one night, and he'd made sure to get his fill.

He lifted the covers, peering down at her still-naked body. His hand was resting on her thigh, covering most of it with his grip. She was petite, but strong. She'd been timid at first; eventually he'd gotten her to loosen up and tell him what she wanted. That was when the real fun had begun.

She stirred in her sleep, wiggling against him, making him groan. He could feel the moment she woke. Her whole body went rigid, her breathing stopped. Like a startled baby deer. "Exhale, Callie. You're seconds away from passing out."

She let out a breath, wrapping his blankets tightly around her naked body as she climbed out of his bed.

"I need to go." She plucked her dress from where it was draped over his desk chair. "I didn't mean to stay the night."

Jasper sat up, grabbing his briefs from the floor, slipping them on as he stood. "It's no big deal. You want me to drive you home?" Another thing he never offered. Driving someone home gave opportunity for talks of brunch and seeing each other again. The way Callahan was racing around his room, searching out her clothes, told him she wouldn't be down for a meal with him at the moment.

"Uh, no, thank you." She pulled on her panties, frowning when she noticed that one side was ripped, making him lick his lips at the memory. "I can order a car. I don't need the whole dorm seeing you drive me home."

She had him there. No telling how many chicks he'd banged in her building. Better to keep things surface and easy. "Okay, cool." He took basketball shorts out of his dirty clothes hamper, stepping into them. "Thanks again for your help this week. I really appreciate it."

"You're welcome. Again." She stood, now fully dressed, her hair looking rather wild around her pretty face. "I, uh, I'm not sure what else I'm supposed to say here. Bye?" She waved, a wince on her face.

He snorted, loving she was completely ill-equipped in the art of one-night stands.

He stepped over a discarded baseball glove, coming to a stop in front of her. He put his palm on her collarbone, wrapping his fingers gently around her neck. "You don't have to say anything at all, but bye works, Callie." He moved his palm up, cupping her cheek before placing a soft kiss to her still slightly swollen lips. "See ya around."

She pulled back, nodded twice, and then turned and walked out the door.

***

Riley drained his bottle of water, then tossed the empty into the sink with a loud crack. "Was that Callahan tiptoeing out of here, holding her shoes?" His hands were on his hips, and he was watching Jasper make his way down the stairs, his expression like a parent scolding a naughty toddler.

"I don't fuck and tell." Jasper smirked, collapsing on the couch and kicking his feet up on the coffee table.

"Yes, you absolutely do." Blake walked down the stairs, ruffling his hair on her way to her mate. "All the time. Even when we ask you to stop." She kissed Riley's lips before moving to the kitchen and rummaging in the fridge.

"Oh, right." Jasper shrugged because his roomies weren't wrong. He was an open book, whether they wanted to read it or not. "Then yeah, that was Callahan, doing the walk of fame."

"*Fame?*" Riley rolled his eyes. Hard. He reminded Jasper of Axie in that moment. "Why didn't you offer to drive her home? I thought Axie and Madden raised your bitch ass better than that."

Jasper knew how Maddi would feel about him letting Callahan stumble out of his house without at least calling her a ride. He was a fuck-boy, not an asshole. "I did offer, she said she didn't want anyone to see us together."

"Ouch."

Jasper waved away Riley's concern. "Nah. I get it. She's all smart and prim and proper. Her friends would think she'd lost her mind, hooking up with me. We're on opposite spectrums of campus, metaphorically speaking."

"Did she teach you what metaphorical meant?" Blake spoke around a handful of blueberries, smiling at him sweetly.

"Yes." He winked. "But don't worry, I taught her some things last night too."

Blake snorted. "You're an actual mess."

"Says the chick who is dropping food all over the floor." Jasper pointed at the ground and the berries rolling under the coffee table. "No one is going to come steal it from you, slow down, killer."

"I'm hungry." Blake tossed a few more into her mouth. "And I'm slightly hungover. I really want a greasy cheeseburger." She jerked a thumb in Riley's direction. "But this one is still on his clean eating kick."

"I never said you had to participate." Riley slung his arm around his mate's neck, pulling her close and kissing her temple. "You want me to go get you a heart attack on a bun, Barbie? Because what my baby wants, my baby gets."

Jasper loved their connection, loved the way they were together. Being around mated pairs was nice, inspirational even. No way he was ready for that sort of connection, but it was still something he aspired to. One day. In the *very* distant future.

"You're the sweetest boyfriend in the history of boyfriends, but I'll live without the grease for one day."

"I'm your mate."

"Yeah, that's what I said." Blake grabbed a banana from the always full bowl of fruit on the kitchen counter and joined Jasper on the couch while ignoring Riley's scowl. "So, you going to hang out with Callahan again?"

Jasper jerked back, appalled. "What? No. Why in the actual hell would I do that?"

"To date." Blake winked at Riley as she put a big portion of her banana in her mouth. "To learn about yourself and other people? Life experience?" Her words were garbled with the food she was chewing.

"Doll face, dating is not really something shifters do." Jasper leaned forward and took a bite, mostly to annoy her. "Knowing there is one perfect person out there, made for us, kind of makes casually hanging out a waste of time."

"And how do you know Callahan isn't your person? Huh?" Blake moved her fruit out of reach when Jasper made another move for it.

He chuckled at her absurd question. "My dick's been inside her. I've touched her. Spent actual time with her. And I wouldn't have cared if she was gone before I woke up." He shook his head. "Not really the feelings I'd have after banging my soul mate."

"Uh, Riley's dick was inside me, and he dropped me off at home the next day. It took weeks of you two growling at each other like a bunch of strays for anyone to know that I was *his* mate."

"That's different." Riley sat on the arm of the couch, tugging on Blake's blonde curls.

She raised one eyebrow. "How so?"

"I liked you from the start. I was drawn to you. I wanted to know you and be next to you and spend time with you. We were inseparable from the moment you blew into my dorm room. Hell, we started having sleepovers that same weekend, whether my dick stayed in my pants or not, I held you all night."

Jasper nodded, recalling how obsessed Riley was with Blake when they'd first met. Every time he'd talked to his best friend on the phone, he was hanging out with Blake or had gotten home from hanging out with Blake. Jasper had been jealous as shit when he thought Blake was a dude. At that point, things were platonic, but that didn't make the connection any less.

"Jasper, are you telling me you weren't drawn to Callahan? You stalked her until she agreed to give you the time of day."

Jasper gasped in outrage. "I did no such thing."

"You followed her around campus, stole her number from your booty call's phone, and then sat at a bar for two hours waiting for her to show up."

"Wrong." Jasper shook his head. "I kept my eye on a hot chick I wanted to fuck. I went to the bar with my bestie, and Callahan just happened to show up. And the digit stealing, well, that one really wasn't my finest moment." He hadn't been stalking her, he'd been pursuing her. That was better, right?

"You told her you needed a tutor." She pointed at herself. "You already had a tutor." Blake wasn't letting it go, and she was starting to make him question his decisions.

"You were busy, and I can't fuck you."

Riley chucked him on the back of the head. "Hey, you promised not to bring that up until January."

"I wasn't recalling a memory. I was stating a fact."

Blake nodded. "I'll allow it."

Riley petulantly crossed his arms over his chest, upset at losing the ruling.

"I really did need the extra help. English lit is hard as fuck. I don't want to fail my freshman year. Jace would never let me hear the end of it, let alone Linc. And Maddi would be so disappointed in me." Jasper was a jokester, rarely serious. That didn't mean he didn't want his pack to be proud of him. "So, two birds, one stone. I got help for the test, and I gave Callahan the dicking she so desperately needed."

Blake rolled her eyes at his crass language, even though her tongue wasn't any cleaner. "Don't act like you did that poor girl any favors."

"I didn't say I did her a favor. I said she needed dick." Callahan was uptight, completely. After they'd been together though, she'd seemed to relax a bit. She let her guard down, she laughed for fuck's sake. She was brilliant, and Jasper knew he'd aced the lit final thanks to her. She had a way of explaining things that made it all click in his brain. "Just because I don't want to date her doesn't mean I'm mistreating her in any way. We agreed to one night before I even touched her. No lies, no drama."

"I think you're selling her and yourself short." Blake got up, tossing her empty banana peel at his head. "She's a cool chick, and I think you're into her." She held her hand up when he opened his mouth to reply. "No need to make a joke about how *into* her you were, I get it."

Jasper pouted. "I need new material or new friends."

Riley grabbed Blake's hips and dragged her over to stand between his knees. "For once, I have to agree with Jasper here, doll." He kissed her frowning lips. "Jasper casually dating Callahan would only hurt her. She isn't meant for him. It's destined to end, no matter what. It's shifter life."

"All *I'm* saying is, you guys could both be wrong." She pointed at Jasper. "You *are* drawn to her, whether you want to admit it or not. You changed your normal gross male routine for her."

"I adapted the play to score the points." Jasper sighed, shaking his head like he was disappointed in himself. "You said it yourself. I never try to hide it. I'm a fuck-boy, it's literally what we do."

"You let her stay the night, and we both know that is not the way you operate."

Jasper snorted. "I didn't let her stay the night, I banged her until neither one of us could move. We didn't sleep, we passed the hell out. As soon as she came to, I showed her the door."

Blake stepped out of Riley's embrace. "I need to go spend some time with Axie, all this damn shifter testosterone is starting to annoy the ever-loving shit out of me."

Jasper gasped playfully. "Do you kiss my packmate with that dirty mouth?"

"Yeah. I suck his dick with it too."

She left both of them laughing as she made her way upstairs.

Chapter Ten

Callahan

Straight As. Not that she was surprised. That was what was expected of her, and it was what she expected of herself. Perfection and decorum in all things. Expect for that time she'd given in and let Jasper make her come until her legs felt like jelly. She placed her palms to her cheeks, trying to hide the blush creeping into her skin. She was walking through campus and she'd needed coffee. She was dragging. She was headed home in a few days, choosing to stay in her dorm until the last day possible. It wasn't that she wasn't excited to see her parents, but she knew the summer that was waiting for her. She'd work in her dad's church doing secretary duties to earn spending money for next semester. She'd have dinner with her parents every night, and she'd escape to the library for a break when she could. Predictable. Boring.

Jasper wasn't boring. She was sure his summer would be filled with parties and hookups and beer bongs. She pictured him in swim trunks doing a back flip off some party barge while people cheered his crazy antics and recorded it for social media. He'd make out with daring girls in skimpy bikinis and forget all about his one night with his repressed English lit tutor.

She wasn't sure why she was getting so down on herself. She wasn't normally like this. Jasper had affected her more than she'd anticipated. Her act of rebellion giving her a small taste of how the other half lived. It'd been over a week since she'd spent time with him, and their final had been one of the earlier ones on campus, so she hadn't even seen him in class. Yet, every night she thought of him as she fell asleep.

"Hey, Callahan, how are you?"

She stopped short, glancing up for the first time since she left the dining hall. "Riley. Hi. I'm good, thanks." She liked Riley. He had a calming presence about him, and he had kind eyes and hair that almost matched hers. Plus, he was so in love with Blake it'd warmed her heart to see them together. "How are you?"

"I'm great, I—" He stopped speaking, his head tilting to the side, reminding her of a dog when they heard an odd noise.

She glanced behind her, then to the side, wondering what had caught his attention. "Uh, are you okay?" He ignored her, his eyes narrowing to the point of almost closing. Her gaze darted around, trying to understand what was causing his odd behavior. "Riley?" She waved her hand in front of his face. "Are you okay?"

He blinked a few times like he was coming out of a trance. "Yep." His smile seemed entirely forced as he popped the "P" on his reply. "And you? You okay? You good?"

She laughed nervously. They'd already gone over the fact that she was good. "I am, yeah." She answered him again because really, what else was she to do? Ask him if he'd lost his mind?

"Finals are intense, feeling tired?" He pointed to the iced coffee in her hands. "Is that straight black coffee on ice? That's a lot of caffeine, huh?"

"Uh, yes, it is." She'd been up late reading, and avoiding packing the last of her belongings. "You know, I should go. I have a big to-do list to complete before I head home this weekend." She pursed her lips as he leaned toward her, his eyes narrowed once again in concentration. "Tell Blake I said to have a good summer." She went to step past him, but he blocked her way, moving even closer to her.

She felt trapped and a little uneasy. They were in the middle of campus. There were plenty of people around she could call out to, which she might have to do since Riley was behaving so strangely.

He kept going into that odd trance-like stare, and then snapping himself out of it. She glanced down at his wrist to see if he was wearing some sort of medical alert bracelet. Nope.

"Callahan, hey, packing, am I right? I saved it all for the last minute and I needed caffeine too." She felt instant relief when one of her dorm neighbors stopped next to them. She motioned between her and Riley. "Oh, sorry I didn't mean to interrupt."

Callahan waved away her neighbor's concern. "This is Riley, he's Blake's boyfriend. She's the pretty blonde in our lit class."

Riley straightened, once again seeming to rejoin reality, and smiled kindly at them both. "It was nice to see you again, Callahan." He sighed, shaking his head as he chewed at his lower lip. "Take care of yourself?"

She nodded, waving as he stepped past her and made his way across the quad.

She was glad that they'd been interrupted. Riley had been acting completely out of character.

If she'd grown closer with Blake, she would've messaged her to make sure he was feeling okay. As it was, she hadn't seen or spoken to Blake since the last time she'd been at their house.

The morning after her sleepover with Jasper.

Chapter Eleven

Jasper

"Hey, man, you got a minute?"

Jasper closed his laptop when Riley walked in and perched on the edge of his messy unmade bed. He'd gotten done FaceTiming Linc, Maddi, and Allison. He missed the hell out of the rest of his pack. Allison was growing so fast, already crawling and pulling up on furniture. Linc and the other coaches ended the season as division champs, again. Now it was time to start recruiting, handpicking the badass ball players who would receive scholarships to St. Leasing for the next school year. A part of him longed to be there with them, watching the submitted game tapes and making a list of names on the whiteboard in Dom's office. A bigger part of him was happy to be where he was, with his best friend, being a normal college freshman. After the time he spent living with Jace, he refused take his freedom in Greenly for granted.

"Yeah, what's up?" Jasper narrowed his eyes, studying his packmate. "You have that serious look on your face, like this is about to be some kind of after-school special."

Riley winced. "You're not far off."

"Huh?"

"Fuck, man, I really don't even know how to start this conversation." Riley's hands were linked behind his head, his gaze on the ceiling, a heavy sigh leaving his lips. "Did you, uh, wrap it up when you were with Callahan?"

Jasper let out a chuckle. "Of course I wrapped it up. I always wrap it up." That was something that was drilled into shifters from a young age. Always use protection. Raw doggin' was for mates only. It was probably the only sacred thing he actually believed in at this point. "Did you really come in here to talk about birth control with me?"

"Speaking of birth control, was uh, is Callahan on the pill?"

"I highly doubt it, bro." She didn't seem like the type of girl who felt the need to take a pill every day when she had sex once every three or four years. Jasper pitched forward and pulled open his nightstand drawer, holding up the giant box of condoms he kept there. "I didn't ask though, because I make sure I'm careful all on my own. What gives?"

Riley bit at his lower lip so hard it turned white. "Did you pull out?"

"Dude, what is with all these questions? What are you getting at here?" Jasper crossed his arms over his gray t-shirt, leaning back in his desk chair. "I was careful. It's literally the only thing in life I take seriously."

"Callahan is pregnant."

Jasper's smirk fell into a gasp. "What? Uh, what did you just say to me?"

"I ran into her today on campus. She's definitely pregnant. I couldn't hear the baby's heartbeat, it's too early. But I can tell, man. I can always tell. She's maybe four weeks?"

Jasper didn't doubt his packmate's ability to notice the changes in Callahan's body. It wasn't the first pregnancy Riley had confirmed before it was *humanly* possible.

Riley was the first to know Corey was pregnant with Hadley. That was how he'd discovered his supernatural talent. He'd honed that skill to a science with every new pregnancy in their pack. Callahan's baby wasn't Jasper's though, it couldn't be, there was no way.

"It's not mine. I was with her no more than two weeks ago. She must've already been pregnant when I banged her." It was a good thing Jasper didn't have Riley's ability. He wasn't sure he would've been able to go through with it if he'd known she was knocked up. "That's a weird thought, huh? Fucking someone else's baby momma."

Riley's forehead wrinkled for a moment, and then his eyes got all big and serious again. "That's not at all how pregnancy timing works. She's maybe four weeks pregnant, that means she got pregnant *two weeks* ago. Which was exactly when she stayed the night here."

Jasper's head cocked to the side. "How does that make any sense?

Riley blinked, incredulous. "Next semester I'm enrolling you in a human biology class." He grabbed Jasper's laptop, opening it and bringing up the calendar they'd shared all semester for school and baseball schedules. "You start counting on the first day of the last period. A cycle is four weeks, you ovulate in the middle of the cycle usually around day—"

Jasper snorted when he saw Blake had labeled the night Callahan had slept over as *Callahan's lapse in judgment.* "Okay, I promise I'll take the biology class. Get to the point you're trying to make."

"Unless she was with someone else the same weekend, that baby is definitely yours." Riley shut the computer and tossed it beside him on the bed, the finality of it jarring inside Jasper's skull.

With someone else? That didn't sound like Callahan.

She wasn't that type of girl, was she? He should probably stop making assumptions about the kind of person she was. It wasn't as if he took the time to get to know her. But then again… No. He knew the answer even if he wished like hell he didn't. That meant the baby…

"Nope."

"Jasper."

He shook his head, unblinking. "No, thank you."

Riley let a few moments of silence stretch between them before leaning forward and getting in front of Jasper's catatonic stare. "Are you okay? You went all pale, are you going to puke?"

"Nuh-uh."

Riley's eyes narrowed. "You aren't going to puke or you're not okay?"

"No way."

"Mmmm'kay." Riley leaned back on one hand, taking out his cell and starting a puzzle game. "I'm going to just, uh, I'm going to sit right here, and when you're ready to talk this out, you let me know. I'm here for you, buddy."

Talk this out? How the hell was he supposed to talk anything out when his brain was having trouble accepting the situation could possibly be real?

His skull felt all tingly and his vision started to blur at the edges. He willed his lungs to keep working, his heart to continue to beat. Dying in this moment would be bad and not something he could come back from.

He was careful, he was always careful. He didn't want to hurt anyone, and he sure as fuck didn't set out to ruin anyone's life. Yet, that was what he'd done, right?

Callahan would be tied to him for the next eighteen years. At least. She'd be forced to raise a kid with him and watch as he met his true mate and settled down. *If* she wanted to keep the baby.

Did she want to keep it? Did he? Jasper wanted kids one day, he did. When he pictured his future family though it was children with his mate, with his forever. This wasn't how it was supposed to go.

This was *not* supposed to happen to him. To her. To them.

He finally found his voice and whispered, "How is this possible?"

"Well—"

"I know how it happened." He got to his feet and started pacing in front of his bed. "I mean, how is it *possible*? I'm a shifter. Shit like this doesn't happen to us. I was *careful*. And she's not my mate.

"What am I supposed to do here? They don't cover this in Shifter 101. I know because Maddi made me take the damn class when Penn started teaching it."

"I wish I had answers for you, bro. I really do." Wouldn't life be so much simpler if Riley could toss him a pamphlet: *What to do when you knock up the wrong chick.* "You want to call Penn? Maybe she'll know more about it."

Jasper shook his head. "I'm not ready for the pack to know." He wasn't ready for anyone to know. He wished *he* didn't fucking know, if he was being honest. "Shit. I need to talk to Callahan."

"She doesn't know yet. It's too early, and like you said, you guys were careful. It's probably not even on her radar. Finals were hectic and now she's packing to move home for the summer." Riley got up, grabbing Jasper's shoulders to stop his frantic pacing.

"So what do I do? Wait for her to come to me? I can't tell her I think she's pregnant because my packmate noticed with his supernatural shifter abilities."

She doesn't know she's pregnant, and she sure as fuck doesn't know she's gotten impregnated by a shifter. Hell, she doesn't even know shifters exist.

Maybe it wasn't his though. Maybe she'd been so into dick after being with him she'd gone out the next night to find another one to hop on? Like a dick addict, searching for her next fix.

Riley dropped his hands to his side now that Jasper was being still. "If it was me, I'd invite her over, see if she's having any symptoms you can notice and point them out. She said she was leaving this weekend, that gives you only a few days to work with. I'm betting it'd be a lot easier for her to find out here on campus than at home with her family waiting for her at the dinner table while she's hurling in the bathroom."

Jasper's eyebrows rose to his hairline. "You're suggesting I follow her around and point out when she starts getting fat? Are you high?"

"How you've survived around four pregnant packmates and not been murdered in your sleep, I'll never know." Riley plucked his laptop from the bed and opened up the internet search engine. "It's way too early for her to start to show, idiot. But there are a ton of pregnancy symptoms that come in the beginning." He turned the screen around. "Nausea, sore breasts, exhaustion, hormonal. If you point things out, maybe she'll start to question things too."

"Whose breasts are sore?" Blake came into the room, plopping down on the bed and wrinkling her nose at the boxer briefs she landed on. "Is someone else pregnant? Oh, is it Axie?"

"It's Callahan."

Blake gasped. "Whoa." She cut her wide disbelieving eyes to Jasper. "You got Callahan pregnant? Are you fucking kidding me?"

"What the fuck, Riley?" Jasper threw his hands in the air. Logically, he knew Riley would tell Blake. Jasper probably would've told her himself as soon as he had a moment to digest it. To blurt it out like that though seemed harsh. "According to your mate's wolf senses, Callahan is the right amount of preggo for the baby to be mine."

"That's so freaking huge. I don't even know what to say. Does she know?"

Both he and Riley shook their heads.

"I ran into her on campus," Riley explained. "It's too early, and there's no way she suspects yet."

Jasper lay down on the bed, curling up next to Blake and closing his eyes. He needed some comfort and cuddles. He'd ended up having a real shit day.

Most likely taking pity on him, Riley ignored their close proximity.

"That reminds me, Barbie Doll. We need to talk about me being your *boyfriend*."

Blake gasped again, this time dramatically fake as fuck as she ran her fingers through Jasper's hair. "Are you breaking up with me?"

"We're mated, we're end game. There is no breaking up."

"Then what's your point, sourpuss?"

Jasper snorted at her nickname for his best friend. Riley could for sure be a sourpuss. No one could bring him out of his funk better than Blake though, a job that used to solely belong to him.

He was glad Riley had changed the subject for a beat; he couldn't wrap his brain around his next steps, and talking it to death wasn't going to help calm his racing heart.

"I don't like being called your boyfriend. I'm more than that. *We're* more than that."

"Uh, okay? What would you like me to refer to you as? BAE? Boo? Lover?" Jasper could hear the smile in her voice. "Oh. I know. We could go old-school. How about concubine? Or paramour?"

"Hilarious." Riley reached out and moved her hand off the top of Jasper's head, clearly fed up with his mate touching another male. "We could tell people we got married."

"If that got back to my parents, they'd probably have some questions."

Riley scoffed. "Your parents love me."

"They love you as my first serious college boyfriend. They'd love you less if they thought we got married after six months of knowing each other." Blake got up and abandoned Jasper, and climbed into Riley's lap.

"Fiancée?"

She wrinkled her nose. "People will think I'm knocked up."

Riley glanced past his mate to grin at Jasper. "Don't worry, soon Callahan will be showing and everyone will be looking at her instead."

"True." They both ignored Jasper's huff of annoyance. Humor at his despair wasn't cool. "All right. We're engaged." She held their hands up, like a bride and groom walking into their wedding reception.

Riley took her face in his hands, staring into her eyes to drive his point home. "We're mated."

"Right, that's what I said."

Jasper drowned out their kisses and whispered words. Usually, he'd give them shit until they either stopped or left his room to go fuck in their own. Tonight, he didn't have the energy.

He felt drained. Emotionally exhausted. He knew about the baby, but Callahan didn't. It was a heavy secret to have. For once he couldn't smile or joke or flirt his way out the mess he'd created.

"I fucked up, didn't I?"

Blake and Riley pulled away from each other, joining him on his bed. Blake went back to rubbing his head and Riley reached out to squeeze his shoulder. "You didn't fuck up, you were careful. Responsible." He paused like he was trying to find the right words. "The cause simply yielded an unexpected outcome."

"You know we're with you all the way. No matter what." Blake tugged lightly on his hair. "How do you want this to play out after you two talk and she knows?"

"She's not meant for me—"

"So you say," Blake interrupted, and Riley put his palm over her mouth to keep her from adding anything else to contradict him.

"How does this even work? We co-parent?" He grabbed a pillow and put it over his face. "That's going to seriously put a damper on all my extracurricular activities."

Blake pulled the pillow out of his grasp. "You need to take this one step at a time right now." She held up a finger. "When Callahan finds out, be supportive and kind. You worked your ass off to convince her that hooking up with you was a good idea. You owe her compassion and patience." She added a second finger to her tick-off. "Figure out what she wants to do, how she wants to handle the pregnancy. And again, your little player ass better be down with whatever choice she makes. Her life changes, no matter what, way more than yours will." She added a third finger. "Then, together, you move forward."

Three steps. That didn't seem so overwhelming. Whereas, thinking about co-parenting and who got the kid for Christmas versus Thanksgiving was about to make him shift into wolf form and never walk on two legs again.

"I should've left her alone." Most likely, he'd never forgive himself for humping that sweet girl. He'd been all cocky in his pursuit, and proud of the conquest. Now he felt sick.

"Jasper, bud, honestly it could've happened to any of us, you know?" Riley shrugged, a sad smile on his face. "You simply had more opportunities than most."

So many opportunities. So very many.

He sighed, closing his eyes once again and resting his forehead against Blake's thigh, taking comfort and warmth from his packmates.

Better Callahan than some of the other chicks he'd been with, he supposed.

If there was a silver lining, it was that he hadn't gotten the chick who thought he was a time traveling Tom Welling pregnant.

Chapter Twelve

Callahan

Callahan still wasn't all the way packed. She wasn't sure what her deal was when it came to leaving campus and heading home. It was as if she couldn't make herself put the last of her things into a suitcase. She knew she couldn't stay on campus. The dorms were closing for renovations and she couldn't afford an apartment without her parents' help. They wouldn't condone her staying away for the next three months. They'd barely let her move away for college in the first place. She was their only child, their pride and joy. She'd never stepped one toe out of line and they cherished her. Her dad was strict and his morals were absolute. Her mom was kind, always trying her best to soften the harshness of her father's rule to no avail.

Callahan had never felt freer than she had this past year at UNC. She'd made her own schedule. She'd eaten when she wanted to and stayed up late if the desire struck her. Sure, she spent more time in her dorm room than out of it, but no one fussed at her when she left her wet towels on the floor. She knew going home, back to having her parents watching her every move, was going to be absolute torture.

She lay back on her twin mattress, staring at her blank ceiling and begging her thoughts not to stray to the incorrigible one-night stand she'd allowed herself. *Jasper.* It wasn't fair. His body was sculpted by the hands of gods.

Muscles on muscles without looking bulky and ridiculous. His smile, or more like his smirk, was stupid sexy. Which was a phrase she never thought she'd use in her life. *Stupid sexy*. Ugh. She scrubbed her hands down her face, seriously considering a nap in favor of packing, when her phone dinged on her crowded desk.

J: *Riley said you were moving home for the summer. Why don't you come have dinner with us before you go? We'd all love to see you.*

Their first communication in two weeks, exactly when she'd been thinking about him and their night together, as if her memories had summoned him. When Jasper promised her one night and nothing more, he'd meant it. She hadn't even seen him around campus.

C: *Dinner? I thought one night and we never spoke again?*

She'd thought of him often, but her urge to contact him had diminished over the past couple of weeks. Hearing from him out of the blue? She couldn't help giving him a hard time, throwing his promise back in his face. She wasn't so much hurt he hadn't reached out before now. What she felt was an emotion she couldn't quite place.

J: *You helped me pull a B in English lit, and Blake keeps asking about you. That deserves an exception to the rule.*

C: *Oh, how gracious thou art.*

J: *Another reason you should come to dinner. You're funnier than I remember. Although, after I got your panties off, we didn't do much talking.*

She would be lying if she said that his reminder about their night together didn't turn her on. But it wasn't why she was agreeing to dinner. She liked Blake and Riley, although he'd been a little odd when they'd run into each other. One group dinner couldn't hurt, right? Jasper didn't sleep with girls more than once. He'd said it and the rumor mill confirmed it. It wasn't as if he was trying to get her back into his bed.

C: *I'm hilarious, I assure you. I'll bring dessert.*

She could stop on the way and grab some cookies. Her mouth watered at the thought of sugar. Sweets weren't something they indulged in much at home, but she'd been sure to have her fair share while she'd been away in Greenly.

J: See you in an hour?

She glanced at her watch and the pile of clothes balanced on her bed. Looked like she got to put packing off for one more day. Dinner was a really good excuse. She thumbs-up'd his text and hopped off her bed to shower. She'd been slow to wake that morning and then spent the majority of her day lying around. She was being lazier than she'd ever been in her life. She didn't seem to have the energy to scold herself about it like she normally would.

Callahan knew the moment she got home her newly sluggish ways wouldn't be tolerated. Her father started his day at seven am sharp, and he expected her and her mother to as well. Ugh. She was already feeling drained and she hadn't even set foot outside of campus life.

***

Blake answered the door, looking beautiful as always. Even when she wore yoga pants and an oversized t-shirt, she was stunning. Her curls and her pouty lips made it appear like she was put together no matter what. "Callahan." Blake pulled her in for a hug, making some of her nerves dissipate. "I'm so glad you came. I've been bugging Jasper to have you over."

Callahan smiled, thrusting the cookies she picked up into Blake's hands. She wasn't sure what to say. Blake wanted her here, but ultimately, Jasper hadn't?

"We ordered some pizza. It'll be here in an hour." Riley took the dessert out of Blake's hands as he joined them. "That sound okay to you?"

She nodded, studying Riley for signs of insanity. All weirdness from their last encounter was gone. He was acting perfectly normal, as if she'd imagined it. "I love pizza, thank you."

He held up the cookies. "Thanks for these. Blake and Jasper will scarf them down like two little vultures."

"If you let us keep more sweets in the house, we wouldn't act like crack addicts when we get to eat them." Jasper came down the stairs, basketball shorts low on his hips, his t-shirt tight on his biceps. "Hey, Callie. I'm glad you came." He put his hand on her shoulder, grasping her neck to pull her into a quick hug. "We were going to sit out back for a bit while we waited on the food. You game?"

She nodded again, not sure why she was having such a hard time using her voice around these people. They were being perfectly nice and welcoming. Maybe Jasper's spicy scent was clouding her brain. He smelled so good—it wasn't fair.

She followed the three of them through the kitchen and out to the back patio. She hadn't seen this part of the house when she'd been there before. They had a large yard with perfect green grass. The fencing was high, higher than the traditional six feet. She noticed there were cameras pointed beyond it as well.

They had a nice concrete patio, outdoor furniture with luxe navy cushions, and string lights giving the space a chill vibe. There was a speaker somewhere she couldn't see, letting music flow from the house. It was crazy that three college students got to live like they did.

"How did the rest of your finals go?" Blake broke the silence, sitting next to Riley and putting her feet in his lap.

"Fine." Callahan smiled, trying hard to not act so uptight. "I finished my last one a few days ago. I've been packing to head home, but mostly, napping and procrastinating. Are you guys staying in Greenly for the summer?"

"Napping? Are you not getting enough sleep for some reason? Feeling tired?" Jasper handed her a bottled water he'd pulled from a refrigerator under an outdoor bar she hadn't noticed until right now.

"Oh, um, yeah I guess." Talking more about her sleeping habits seemed like an odd way to steer the conversation.

"We're staying in Greenly for the most part. Perk of living off campus." Thankfully Blake saved them again. "Rye and I will go visit my parents at some point, and we're making a trip back to Haxton to hang with his family for a while too."

Callahan sat up straighter, cracking her neck from side to side as she arched her back. Her shoulder, her lower back, every part of her had felt a bit achy over the last couple of days. She glanced to the side, finding Jasper staring at her chest. Had she been wrong to think he wouldn't try to hook up with her again? He was checking out her breasts, not seeming to care she'd caught him in the act.

"So you're moving home? What'll you do there?" Blake was seriously saving her, over and over again. Riley wasn't speaking, he was doing that thing where he kind of stared off into space in her general direction, and Jasper was being skeevy.

"I'll work for my dad. He's a pastor, I'll answer phones and that kind of thing." She shifted in her seat, turning to face Blake more fully while trying to hide her cleavage from Jasper. "Pretty boring summer, to be honest."

"Your father is a pastor? I didn't know that." Blake kicked Riley, seeming to bring him out of his trance. "Did you hear that, babe? Callahan was telling us her father is a pastor."

"Wait." Jasper perked up, no longer unashamedly staring at her chest. "What?"

"Yeah. It's true. My father's been a pastor my entire life." She didn't really want to talk about her father with the guy she'd had a one-night stand with, but for the life of her, she couldn't figure out how to gracefully change the subject. "The church has about two hundred members, so there's a lot of clerical work that goes along with the whole pastor thing. That's where I come in."

"So religious, then. You grew up religious." Jasper steepled his fingers, resting his chin on them. "Is that safe to say? Lots of convictions."

"Uh, I guess. Yeah. I grew up going to church every Wednesday and Sunday. Bible study and Sunday school, the works." She cleared her throat. "I, as most people do, have convictions, yes." She was quickly regretting her decision to come over. Riley and Jasper were acting strange and Blake was doing her best to make up for it. Callahan was feeling sleepy again, like another nap was warranted.

"Is he a big man, your father? Anger issues?"

"No." Callahan stood, setting down her water on the glass table beside her. "I'm going to use the restroom, if that's okay?" She didn't wait for anyone to answer her. She needed a reason to walk away from the world's weirdest conversation.

Maybe she could hide in there until the pizza came.

Chapter Thirteen

Jasper

As soon as Callahan had disappeared into the house, Blake leaned forward and flicked Jasper on the forehead. "You two need to get your actual shit together." She shook her head. "You're acting looney tunes." He knew she was right. She'd been the one who steered the conversation as best she could, but she wasn't a miracle worker.

Riley had zoned out, checking in on the pregnancy and, more than once, Jasper had found himself staring at her perfect and growing tits. He wondered if they would keep growing. He wanted to hold them in his palms and note the difference in their weight. Did they hurt yet? Were they tender? Extra sensitive? He wanted to run his tongue around her nipples and ask if it felt different than the night they'd shared. How was he going to bring up the size of her breasts without making her angry and causing her to storm out of the house?

Callahan probably thought they were all insane.

"She's still pregnant." Blake turned to look at her mate like he'd lost his mind. "What? Things happen, especially early on." Riley pulled a beer from the tiny outdoor fridge that'd been here when they'd moved in. Jace had renovated the whole place without their input.

"Stop zoning out while you stare at her." Blake pointed to Riley. "And you," she glared at Jasper, "stop gawking her breasts and asking her dumb questions about her father." She was whisper-yelling at them, which was warranted.

"Did you hear her though? She grew up going to church two days a week and her father is a pastor." Jasper let his head fall back against the side of the house. "We can guess how she'll feel about abortion."

Riley scoffed. "Yeah? How do you feel about it?"

"I don't know. I've never been in this position before."

"Exactly." Riley handed him his beer, allowing him to drain it in solidarity. "You never know how you'll react until it happens to you. So stop assuming things about her by the way she was raised."

"This is a cluster fuck." Blake crossed her arms over her chest, clearly still irritated with the both of them. "We'd have been better off telling her you're both shifters and you noticed she was preggo with your Spidey senses."

They all stopped talking when Callahan came back into view. She stepped on the back patio, an uneasy smile on her face. "I think the pizza is here, someone was knocking at the door."

"Thank goodness." When the bell rang, they all filed into the house and Blake skipped to the door like a little blonde pixie. She took the pizza boxes in her hands and then rested her cheek against the top of the grease-stained box. "Oh, how I've missed you."

Riley shook his head as he handed a wad of cash to the delivery man, who was watching Blake's declaration with interest. Riley slammed the door in the guy's face, then followed his mate into the kitchen, smacking her ass playfully.

"Do you smell that?"

"Yeah. I know it smells so good. This is our favorite pizza place." Jasper pulled four plates down from the cabinet, even though Blake was already shoving a slice into her mouth. "Let's eat."

Callahan put her hand over her mouth. "You don't smell that?" Her voice was muffled from her palm while her fingers were pinching her nose closed. "It smells awful. What kind of pizza is that?"

Jasper cut his gaze to Riley who was pulling a pepperoni- and jalapeno-filled slice from the box. Riley's eyes widened, his head gesturing to Callahan. She didn't like the smell of the pizza. Jasper had read about food aversion on the website Riley had sent him. It was a symptom. A sign. It was better than her knocked up boobs, or questioning her napping habits, that was for fucking sure.

"You okay? You look like you're going to be sick." Jasper reached out, touching her forehead, and not caring when she swatted away his hand in annoyance. "No fever."

"I'm not sick." She wrinkled her nose. "That pizza smells rotten."

"We'll, uh, take it upstairs and eat in our room." Riley picked up one of the grease spot dotted boxes and then grabbed a protesting Blake and hauled her upstairs. Jasper could hear her whining about wanting to stay as their door clicked shut.

Callahan visibly shivered. "I should go and let you eat with your friends, maybe I'm coming down with a stomach bug."

"No." His words came out more forceful than he'd intended, but this was his only shot. She left to go home tomorrow, and he needed her to realize what they'd done. What he'd done. Fuck. Once she knew, there was no denying it anymore. She'd take a test and the answer would be right in front of them, undeniable.

"Stay, I'll make us something else to eat."

"You cook?"

"Well, I reheat." He stood, knowing she'd pull her hand away if he tried to help her up, and headed into the kitchen. "What sounds good? We have leftover chicken, some sweet potato ground turkey mess—"

"Do you have any chocolate syrup?"

Jasper snorted into the fridge, hiding his humor. Nothing about this was funny, it really wasn't. But knowing that she was pregnant and asking for chocolate for dinner was comical. "You want chocolate syrup for dinner? Not very responsible of you, Callie."

"Don't call me Callie." Perched on a bar stool, she reminded him once again that she wasn't a fan of the nickname. "And bananas. Do you have any bananas? Oh, or peanut butter?"

Chocolate syrup, peanut butter, and bananas. Great. His baby momma was going to gain five hundred pounds and he'd have to wheel her into the hospital like a barrel. He grabbed all three ingredients and sat them in front of her, trying to keep his expression as blank as possible. "Not a pizza fan?"

"I love pizza, it's just that pizza smelled bad. Your friends are probably going to get food poisoning."

He watched as she peeled the banana then dipped it into the jar of peanut butter before drizzling chocolate syrup on top. She took a huge bite and worked to chew around it all. How was he supposed to segue into: *Btdub, I knocked your fine ass up*? He wished Axie were here. She was nicer than Blake. Blake would laugh in his face, but Axie would help him steer the conversation with humor dancing in her eyes like a wicked little minx. *Axie*. That was it. Simply thinking her evil name had given him an idea. She was a bear when she was about to start her period and she ate the weirdest shit. It was perfect.

"PMS-ing?"

Callahan put her hand to her perky expanding chest, swallowing around a mouthful of her banana concoction. "Excuse me?"

"When my sister is PMS-ing, she eats some crazy stuff. Once she melted Hershey's chocolate bars over an entire container of goldfish crackers."

"Uh, not that it's any of your business, but I..." Callahan stared at him for a few moments, then looked down at the half-devoured banana in her syrup-covered hand, her face paling before his eyes. "I, uh, I..." She dropped the banana then put her clean hand over her mouth. "I think I'm going to be sick."

Jasper reached into a cabinet and grabbed their vomit bowl. Why they kept it in the kitchen and continued to use it for popcorn, he'd never understand. Callahan gaped at him like he'd lost his mind, then jumped off the stool and ran to the bathroom and slammed the door in his face when he tried to follow her. He also didn't understand why he'd tried to follow her into the room. Who wants to watch someone else vomit?

Even without supernatural ability, he could hear her puking. She was the loudest puker he'd ever heard, and that was saying something because Blake didn't hold back. A stomach bug had run through the three of them when they first moved in together and he and Riley still made fun of her for the acoustics.

Riley's bedroom door opened at the top of the stairs, his head poking out and his gaze meeting Jasper's.

He shrugged, resigned that his night was going to suck giant donkey dick. A puking chick was in their bathroom and when she came out, he was going to have to convince her to take a pregnancy test. Riley sent him a small smile and then pulled the door closed as Blake tried to stick her head out too.

"Hey, Callie, you okay?"

The toilet flushed, then the water turned on in the sink. A few minutes later, she walked out, a confused frown on her pretty freckled face. "I'm sorry, I should head home. I don't want to get you sick. Hopefully, it's only a twenty-four-hour thing."

Try a nine-month thing.

Jasper was sure him reminding her about her period would've done the trick. She was late by now, if only a day or two. She didn't like the smell of the pizza, she was scarfing down weird shit and then throwing it up. Plus, the boob thing. "What if it's not a stomach bug?"

"The flu? Nah, it's summer and it's not going around campus." She stepped past him and grabbed her bag, slinging it over her shoulder and placing a hand on her stomach like she was feeling nauseous again.

Okay. For a brilliant chick she was being super fucking slow on the uptake here. Damn Riley and his supernatural abilities. She was moving toward the door and with every step she took Jasper was losing his nerve to confront their situation.

Riley stuck his head back out of his bedroom door again, glaring down at him from the second story like he heard Jasper chickening out through the walls. He gestured with his head to the retreating red-haired beauty. Ugh. So he and Blake were listening to Jasper flounder through the door. Fantastic. Exactly what he needed, an audience.

"Callahan, wait."

"I'm feeling pretty crappy, Jasper, I need to go lie down." Her hand was on the doorknob, her back to him.

He hung his head, closing his eyes and steeling his nerves. He'd done this, and it was up to him to figure out where they went next. Fuck-boy or not, this was his responsibility and he didn't want her to be alone when she found out when she could be with him instead.

"Could you possibly be, uh, fuck." She turned to face him and he took a deep, fortifying inhale. "Could you be pregnant?"

Chapter Fourteen

Callahan

Callahan paused with her hand on the door, her heart beating so hard she could see her shirt jump with the motion. *Pregnant.* She closed her eyes, swaying slightly at the suggestion, knowing deep down Jasper could be right. Knowing in that instant that there was a possibility. The pizza smelled disgusting, but the banana-peanut butter-chocolate thing had been delicious. Until Jasper's PMS comment had made it turn to ash in her mouth. She was late, one day late. She never paid attention to her period, there wasn't ever a reason. She didn't have sex. She didn't hook up with hot, cocky player types on a whim. Until Jasper.

"Callahan, look at me, please."

His voice was soft, almost like he was apologizing with every word. She was afraid to meet his gaze, afraid of what she would find. Would he blame her? Would he be as terrified as she was?

She dropped her hand and let her bag fall off her shoulder. "I could be, maybe. Probably not though." She was currently praying for a stomach bug. The worst stomach bug in the history of stomach bugs. She'd take days of feeling sick, of throwing up, if it meant that she wasn't a pregnant college freshman. If it meant her life wasn't about to be over before it ever really started. "We were careful."

They were careful, they were responsible. Except... No, they weren't. Responsible wasn't hooking up with a random guy you barely knew. She'd behave the complete opposite of the kind of responsible she'd been raised to be. When it came to Jasper, she'd been reckless.

Jasper's smile was sad, and so very small. He stepped toward her, picking up her bag and then taking her hand in his. "One step at a time, okay?" For once she didn't pull away from his attention, she welcomed the kind gesture. "We'll go get a test, and then we'll lock ourselves away in my bathroom. Away from offensive-smelling pizza and vomit-inducing banana combinations."

Despite herself, she grinned as she let him lead her out of the house into the cool dark night. It was summer in Colorado, which meant the temperature tended to drop with the sun. The cool air felt good against her heated skin. "Why are you being so calm?" She climbed into his truck after he opened her door, instantly enveloped in his yummy smoke and spice scent. "Why are you being so nice to me?" Jasper buckled her seatbelt and then shut her in the silent vehicle. He didn't answer as he backed them out of the driveway. So she tried a third question. "Why aren't you freaking out?"

"How do you know I'm not freaking out? And I'm being nice to you because neither one of us did anything wrong. We weren't being irresponsible, or stupid, or careless." Jasper seemed to read her thoughts as he used his blinker to turn out of the quaint neighborhood he lived in with Riley and Blake.

"Maybe it's nothing." She hoped it was nothing. She hoped that this was one of those scares you recall as a distant memory or as a cautionary tale. An anecdote from the one time in her life when she did something sexy and bold.

"Yeah, maybe."

They rode the rest of the way in silence. Jasper told her to stay in the truck, that he would go get the test. From the moment she'd thrown up in his bathroom, he'd been surprising her at every turn. He was no longer staring at her breasts or asking weird questions about her childhood. He'd taken on a quiet confidence she found entirely too appealing. Jasper the fuck-boy was easy to ignore, but Jasper as the man he was currently showcasing? Wow.

She watched through the large picture windows as the young cashier giggled and made eyes at the potential father of her possible baby. She was mildly annoyed and slightly jealous. Though she couldn't blame the girl. Callahan knew how gorgeous he was, how his muscles looked in his t-shirt, and the way his shorts sat on his hips. Jasper was magnificent; trying to deny it was futile. She couldn't help but laugh when the girl went utterly still as Jasper placed a pregnancy test on the counter, all signs of flirting gone.

He paid and exited the store. She watched his face, trying to figure out how he was feeling. Why wasn't he freaking out like she was? Maybe his insides were a tangled mess of butterflies and nerves and he was good at not showing it. She wondered if his hands shook as he picked out the test for her.

"Okay. I got the lines one because the internet said the digital ones can be glitchy." He tossed a pink box into her lap before buckling up.

She looked down, wrinkling her nose at the offensive pink color. Not all females liked pink. This pregnancy test would forever change two people's lives; therefore, it should be gender neutral. Or white. Blank. It was what you wanted it to be. Pink implied a hopeful woman, desperate to be pregnant.

Callahan would be praying for the opposite.

"Thank you."

"You don't need to thank me for buying you a pregnancy test." Jasper veered right, making his way back to his home, only a few minutes away. "It's the least my dick can do. Hindsight, I should've bought you the morning-after pill."

The way he spoke was so foreign. The casual way he used crass words. She grew up surrounded by people who didn't cuss, didn't drink, gamble, or dance. They didn't have sex with someone they weren't married to, let alone dating. They certainly didn't buy morning-after pills.

She hadn't even realized she'd been rebelling against her upbringing until that moment, sitting next to a hot guy with a pregnancy test sitting like an anvil in her lap. When had she become so oblivious to her own life choices?

Silly girl, moving forward like every day was guaranteed.

Jasper pulled the truck into the driveway, then shut off the engine. He didn't make a move to get out, or rush her to do so either. He was calm, steady. So unlike the boy he'd been when they'd slept together. "Let me know when you're ready."

"I don't think I'll ever be ready." She tapped the slender box against her open palm, sending him a sliver of a smile. "But maybe it's nothing."

Chapter Fifteen

Jasper

It wasn't nothing. If, for another few minutes, allowing her to believe that helped get her through... Hell, why not? Jasper nodded in agreement. When she finally found the courage to get out of the truck, he waited for her near the still-warm hood. He put his hand on the small of her back, leading her up the front steps. She was allowing him to touch her, which showed how freaked out she was. He'd texted Riley while he was inside the drugstore, asking him and Blake to stay out of sight. Tonight was going to be tough enough without having anyone else bear witness.

He knew Callahan was pregnant. Riley wasn't wrong. He supposed a small part of him was holding out hope though, hope that maybe she'd say it wasn't his. Admit that she'd been with someone else that weekend. He knew it was a long shot. Into casual hookups...Callahan was not. That's what brains do though, right? Push against logic until there is nothing else to put misguided hope in.

Jasper led her upstairs and into his room, shutting and locking the door behind him. He sat down on the edge of his bed, thankful that he'd made it for once. Neither one of them spoke as she went into his bathroom, closing the door with a soft click.

He pulled out his phone, trying to distract himself from, well, everything.

R: You guys are home already?

J: Yeah. She's taking the test now.

R: How is she?

J: Quiet. Nervous. She'll barely look at me.

R: I'm really proud of the way you're handling this for her.

J: I've had time to freak out, pace around the house and lose my shit. It's her turn. I'll be whatever she needs me to be.

R: Let me know if you need us.

J: Thanks man.

Riley was proud of him for being kind? How much of a douche was he usually that basic human decency was getting him stickers on his star chart? Fuck. He tossed his cell onto his desk and ran his hands through his hair. He needed a haircut. Usually, Axie would buzz it for him when he went home. *Home.* Shit.

His pack was going to kill him.

He looked up as the bathroom door opened. Callahan came out, the test in her hand, her lip worrying between her teeth. "It's supposed to take two minutes." She glanced at the clock beside his bed. The same one she'd giggled at when she spent the night. "Good thing you have those giant red numbers to tell us when it's time, huh?"

Jasper patted the mattress next to him. "Come here, Callie." He knew she didn't love the nickname, but he also knew she didn't hate it. It was growing on her, like he was. After she sat next to him, he put his arm around her shoulders. She handed him the test and rested her head on his shoulder.

"I'll never forget how nice you were tonight, no matter what the test says."

He kissed her forehead, unable to stop himself from comforting her. She smelled like apples dipped in candy, and she felt good in his arms. He liked her.

He liked her brilliance and her freckles. He liked that she didn't fall at his feet. He liked that she demanded more from him than his normal bullshit. He liked her long silky hair and her tiny soft hands. Everything about her was a contrast to him, and he appreciated their differences. The true reason he wasn't freaking out was because she made him feel capable, solid, and strong.

Grounded.

His normal antics would be wrong.

He needed to be more, for her.

For both of them.

"It's been two minutes." Her head was still on his shoulder, his arm still holding her tight. She was shaking, like chills were wracking her small body. His heart hurt for her, for them both. "Can you look?" she whispered. "I can't, uh, I don't—"

"It's positive." He didn't bother to check the test, there was no need. In that instant he heard it, the soft flutter, the whoosh of the baby's heartbeat. It was almost as if its mother's knowledge had kick-started it into existence.

His wolf woke up, for the first fucking time since he'd met Callie. He could feel it coming to, sensing what had happened. He held his breath, waiting to see what it would do, how it would feel. *Notice the baby, you dense animal.* Oh great. The damn thing was happy about the pregnancy. He preened, like he'd done a good job. Fucking fantastic.

Callahan began to cry, and he held her tighter while telling his wolf to fuck the hell off. If he wasn't going to be anything but smug, he didn't want his input.

He wasn't sure how long they sat there on his bed, the only sound in the room her tears. He shed a few too. Not for himself, but for her. For the fear she must be feeling, the uncertainty, and the regret.

He should've left her alone. She didn't want him, not at first. He'd pursued her, he'd demanded her attention. He'd played the perfect part, been exactly who she needed him to be to say yes.

What he'd done to them wasn't fair. He vowed in that moment to do it again though. To play the perfect part, to be exactly who she needed him to be in this too. She needed support, and he'd give it. She needed validation, and he'd offer it. Whatever it was that she asked of him, he'd deliver. It was the least he could do, and less than she deserved.

"I don't know if I have any tears left." She wiped at her pretty eyes with both hands, sitting up and pulling away from him. "I'm sorry."

"What exactly are you apologizing for? Emotions? You're human. Tears? You just learned something life-altering."

"We. *We* learned." She sighed. "I haven't even given you a chance to react." Thank goodness Riley told him first. Otherwise, he'd have been repeating different variations of the word *no* over her head as she cried her eyes out against a stunned statue. "Can you tell me how you're feeling?"

"I'm feeling, uh, uncertain, I guess." He reached behind her to his desk to pluck a Kleenex from the box. "I'm not trying to be insensitive or piss you off, but I need you to tell me this is mine."

She narrowed her eyes slightly, pausing to blow her cute button nose. "It's yours."

Her words were like a blow to his gut, killing that last tiny shred of hope he'd been clinging to. He'd known. He'd always known. Hearing the words out loud though, it was more jarring than he thought it would be.

He nodded, when what he wanted to do was bury his body under the covers and never come out. "I figured, I just, I guess I needed to hear it, you know?" He took a deep breath, letting it out slowly. "Okay. I think maybe we just take a beat. Take a few days and absorb this, figure out where we want to go from here."

"Like to keep the baby or not?" She was frowning again, in that way she had that made her appear confused and a little bit sad. "Do you want to be, I mean, will you be…" Her eyes welled up with tears again, spilling down her cheeks, one after the other.

"I'll be here. No matter what you choose." He meant that. He meant it with his whole heart. In a way, it was easier for him. He was always going to play a supporting role in this situation. She had to make the hard choices. The choices he wasn't sure he'd ever have the courage or guts to make.

Chicks had it tough, and anyone who said otherwise was a fucking asshole. "Like I said, let's take a few days, okay? Maybe you can talk through things with your family and—"

"Oh my god, my family."

"I know." The dread on her face made him chuckle in solidarity. "My family is going to flip the fuck out too." Oddly enough, when he thought of his family's reaction to the news, it wasn't his mom and stepdad who came to mind. It was his pack. His chosen family. He worried that Linc and Maddi would be disappointed in him. He wondered if Molly would cry, and if Dom would pop him on the back of the head in that fatherly way he did to all the boys. Would Jace sigh in exasperation? Would Axie ever be able to pick her jaw up off the floor?

"No, you don't understand, my father. What we did was a sin and a child born out of wedlock is blasphemy. They're going to disown me, or hide me in a basement until I give birth." Callahan stood, pacing much like he'd done when Riley had first told him. "I can't be pregnant. I can't."

"Okay, um, well, there are other options. I'll help you. I'll go with and take care of you, I'll do whatever—"

"Didn't you just hear what I said? My parents would disown me."

"For having the baby? Or not having the baby? I'm confused here."

"Both." She wrung out her hands, clenching and unclenching her fists. "They're going to make me have the baby. They're going to make me choose adoption." Her hand went to her forehead, like her thoughts were coming so rapidly that she was having a hard time keeping up. "I'll have to miss a year of school. I'll fall behind. I have to move home. They'll hide me in the house, best-case scenario. Otherwise, they'll send me off to my aunt. She lives all the way down in Florida, but it's far enough away that no one from the church would find out."

"Stop." Jasper stood, putting his hands on her hips to make her stand still. "Stop spiraling and slow down." He moved his palms to her cheeks, making sure she was hearing him. "Your parents don't get to tell you what to do, or what *not* to do. You're eighteen. We're legally adults, Callahan, they have no say in any of this."

"But they're my parents."

"And we would be parents if…" *Whoa.* That was like a baseball bat to the gut to say that out loud. He forged ahead, not wanting her to know his knees had gone weak. "We choose what happens next."

Jasper wasn't sure when he'd decided that Callahan's parents could fuck the hell off. It was most likely somewhere around forcing adoption and locking her in a basement. Intentional or not, he and Callahan were a team. They were in this together. He'd be damned if he let anyone back her into a corner and force her to make a decision she wasn't comfortable with.

"School is over. I live on campus. I have to go home for the summer." She wriggled out of his grip and started her pacing again. "I guess I could hide it for a few months. I won't show until next semester. Maybe I could get another semester of school in before I'd need to take time off." She stopped, biting at her lip. "If we keep the baby. If I keep—"

"We." Jasper vowed to be a good guy through this, and a good guy would say *we* and he'd mean it. So that's what was happening. "We." Huh, the second time wasn't nearly as terrifying. He found that he *did* mean it.

"What do you want to do?"

He wanted none of this to be happening. It was selfish, and it made him feel sick to his stomach. He didn't want to have a baby at nineteen with a girl, who, although amazing, wasn't his true mate. She wouldn't understand that, so he went with a safer answer. "I want to give you the space and time to decide what *you* want to do. I'll be here for whatever you choose. You want to have this baby, then I'll help. We'll take turns with class and school. We'll work out a good schedule and make sure we both graduate. My family is going to lose their shit, but they'll help us too." They sure as hell wouldn't try to lock anyone in a basement. "If you don't want to do this—"

"Adoption?"

Jasper wasn't locked in on how he felt about adoption. Would he be okay knowing their kid was out there, living somewhere else? Maybe they could have an open adoption, maybe they could get updates, to make sure it was okay? Shit. *No.* If it was a boy, they'd have to choose a shifter couple. They'd have to find someone who would know what was coming, would be able to teach them about shifter life and culture. His wolf metaphorically picked his head up again; he wasn't thrilled with Jasper's train of thought. He didn't want the baby with someone else. Not that Jasper cared what his wolf thought one way or another.

Would he need to tell Callahan what he really was? He'd cross that bridge when they came to it. It didn't matter right now. All that mattered in the moment was making sure she knew no one could force her to do anything she wasn't comfortable with.

"Sure. If you want to choose adoption, then I'll be right next to you the whole time. We'll find a great couple, together."

"I have to go home." She looked at the bag he'd already packed to visit his pack, like his suitcase reminder her all over again. "I'll have to lie to them, every day."

"I'm guessing that's also a sin? What do you think will shock them more? The pregnancy, or finding out you lost your virginity at church camp when you were seventeen?"

"Don't make fun."

"I'm not." He was pointing out how ridiculous it was that a grown brilliant woman was so worried about disappointing mommy and daddy. His smirk fell when she started to cry all over again. Was this the shock of the news? Or were these already pregnancy hormones? He doubted she'd appreciate him asking.

"You don't *have* to go home." It was foreign to him that she felt so trapped by her parents' wishes and demands. He'd never been a slave to anyone. For the most part, he'd always been free to make his own choices in life. He'd been living away from his mom and stepdad since he was fifteen. This was Callahan's first venture into the real world, and he'd done her the favor of knocking her up. He was a real gem.

"Yes I do. I live on campus. Dorms close in two days."

"Come stay with me." His eyes widened at his own words. *Whoa.* Where the fuck had that come from? She barely tolerated him, and he wanted her to live with him for the summer?

"I can't stay with you."

"Because your parents' basement is a better option?" The basement wasn't funny anymore. It was now something that pissed him off. Fuck her parents. "Look, you need the space to decide what to do, and I can give it to you. Let me help. Tell your parents you're doing mission work or some shit." The look she sent him was disapproving if not droll, so he added, "I'll let you read me the bible every night, as long as you do it naked." He waggled his eyebrows playfully. "I mean, I can't knock you up twice, right?"

"You're going to get struck by lightning."

She wasn't wrong. He wouldn't be surprised if one day the almighty smote him. He also wasn't joking. He wanted to see those pregnancy boobs up close and real personal. The damage was done. What was the harm in making the best of a difficult situation? Plus, he hadn't been with anyone else since that night with Callie and he was hella horny.

He gave himself a mental head shake, silently telling his dick to back down.

Thankfully his lazy wolf had decided to go back to sleep and he didn't have to deal with his desires at the same time as trying to navigate this emotional minefield.

"One of my paaaa…eople is a nurse." Using the word pack to talk about his family probably wasn't wise if he wanted to keep Callie in the dark as long as possible. "Over the summer she does free physicals on campus for all the public school kids in Haxton. It's not church based, but you could fib a little and tell your parents you're doing god's work." If god's work involved ball sacs and a perpetually jealous Linc.

"You want to take me home for the summer?"

"No, no fucking way." Jasper shook his head quickly. "We'll be *here,* but you could tell your parents you'd be *there*."

"Why can't we go with your family? You want me to lie to mine, why can't we lie to yours? I could really help with the clinic and spend the summer trying to decide what to do about the baby. I'd feel better about everything if it was at least partially true." She sighed, shrugging sadly. "The distraction would help too. I'd go crazy sitting around your house all day with nothing to do but think."

The trouble with taking Callahan's pregnant ass home was his pack would know instantly. If Jasper could hear the baby's heartbeat, then all the other males would be able to as well.

He supposed he could tell them she was a friend, and he was helping her out through this situation.

Would they buy that?

He wasn't really the type of guy to take a random pregnant chick under his wing. He was a self-proclaimed fuck-boy, for fuck's sake.

But.

Maybe they could pass her off as Blake's friend, and make this all Blake's idea.

That could work.

He'd need to convince Blake and Riley to go along with it.

He'd need his wolf to keep his opinions to himself. Not to mention, he'd need to keep his paws off Callahan. Damn.

It was going to be a long-ass summer.

Chapter Sixteen

Callahan

Her gut was swirling. The combination of nerves and uncertainty would make her sick again if her stomach wasn't already empty. She was pregnant. *Pregnant.* Thinking the word made her shiver, like a ghost story told in the dark. She'd been away from home for less than a year and she'd already messed up her life, her plans, her future. It was forever altered. Although she resented a lot of her upbringing, some things stuck no matter how hard she tried to shake them. She was so unsure of what she wanted to do. Her every thought was clouded by a haze of her parents' impending disappointment.

"Okay, Haxton for the summer it is."

Jasper's words jarred her away from her thoughts. Now her stomach was aching for another reason. She barely knew Jasper, and his family were strangers to her. She tried to be brave, but the little girl in her heart was afraid of being away from everything she knew. It'd been her idea, and it would make her feel slightly better about deceiving her father. Still, her nerves were growing jumpier by the second.

"I, uh, I need to finish packing up my dorm room." Her exhaustion lately made sense now. "Can I store some of my stuff here? My dad was supposed to come load everything up tomorrow evening." Ugh. She needed to call her parents, convince them that this last-minute summer *mission* was a good idea. She'd never lied to her parents before. Not that she could remember, and definitely not about something so huge. "I should go." Her gaze cut to the still-closed bedroom door. The process of leaving, driving the short distance to her dorm, and walking up all those stairs made her sleepy, her eyes suddenly wanting to close.

"I'll come by tomorrow morning and help you pack. You can call your parents then too." Jasper took her by the shoulders and spun her around, backing her up until she had no choice but to sit on the edge of his bed. "Tonight, you need sleep."

"I can't stay here with you." She moved to stand and he put his hand on the top of her head, keeping her down. He'd been touching her a lot. It had stopped bothering her, even though she acted as if it did. Now, she was simply too emotionally exhausted to scold him.

"Why? It's not like you haven't done it before." He snorted, reaching around her back and unhooking her bra without getting under her shirt or even looking. The weight of her breasts without the support of her bra was excruciating. Now that she had the two-lined truth staring her in the eye, all the symptoms she'd been ignoring the past day or so became glaringly obvious.

"That was before, and for a whole different reason."

"Callie, come on. I'm not going to try anything with you tonight." He pulled her bra through the armhole of her shirt and tossed it over the back of his desk chair. "You look like you're seconds away from passing out, and our lives just turned on a dime. Surprisingly, sex is the last thing on my mind." He dragged back the covers, patting his mattress, which, she knew from experience, was more comfortable than the twin in her dorm room. "If you go back to your room exhausted and alone, you're going to start crying all over again." He wasn't wrong, and it was annoying. "Sleep, Callie. I'll take you to the dorm in the morning."

"I guess Shakespeare was right, huh?" Her words were whispered and low, almost like she was speaking only to herself. "Lust is madness and only ends with regret."

She met his gaze head on, letting him see the sadness and despair in her own. They'd been warned, the first time they were alone together, they'd been warned what would happen if they gave in. It was as if the universe had provided them with foreshadowing, and like so many, they'd simply ignored it.

"Callie, sleep. Things always seem better in the morning."

She seriously doubted that was true for their situation, but she scooted back, letting him pull the covers over her body. His kindness was appreciated, and she was too worn out to argue. "Where are you going?" After he tucked her in and plugged her phone into his charger like a modern-day gentleman, he moved to the door.

"I need to call my family, let them know we're moving home for the summer." He gestured to his bags by his closet. "I was going to go for a quick visit, but now..." He let his words trail off. "I need to take care of a few things, but I'm not leaving the house. I'll be downstairs if you need anything."

He brought her comfort, there was no denying that. His scent, his sheets, all his things crowding the room. Jasper made her feel better. He made tonight less terrifying. In a million years, she wouldn't've ever expected him to be this way.

She was grateful for him. So incredibly grateful for him.

"Good night."

"Good night, Callie."

He turned off the lights, then tugged the door closed, blanketing her in darkness. Silent tears started to fall the moment she was alone.

Knowing Jasper would be back soon, that he'd crawl in beside her, helped. She felt less isolated.

He'd known she needed him, needed him to get through the night. He'd known exactly what to say, exactly what to do.

In a surprising turn of events, he'd been everything she needed him be.

Chapter Seventeen

Jasper

Regret. Callahan's delicately spoken words had pierced his heart. She seemed so sad, so hopeless and lost. He'd done that to her. His demands and desire. He sighed, pulling his bedroom door closed with a soft click. He knew his friends would be waiting for him. He could hear them moving around the house, putting away food and locking up for the night. Jace had bought this house as an investment, then armed it to the teeth before allowing the three of them to move in. His twin had always taken security seriously, but it'd gotten even more over the top now that he was the new king of the shifter underworld.

Jasper walked slowly down the stairs. He was as tired as Callahan. He felt emotionally spent. He felt like he'd had a grueling workout, not a conversation with a petite redhead.

"Hey." Blake came out of the kitchen, a sympathetic pout on her lips. "How is she?"

"Exhausted. Scared. Sad. All the things you'd expect." He collapsed on the couch, leaning his head back and scrubbing his hands over his face. He needed a shave. He'd been existing in a daze since Riley had dropped the news about the pregnancy. "She's sleeping now, hopefully. I'm going to take her home in the morning and help her pack up her dorm room."

"What does she want to do about the baby?" Riley came in, wiping his hands on a dishtowel.

Without fail, he did the dishes every night before bed. Corey said she'd raised him to be a good mate, a mate with manners. Both Blake and Jasper were reaping the benefits of Corey's hard work.

"As expected, it seems abortion is out, but she's talking adoption. Maybe. I don't think she really knows yet." He pulled his phone from his jogger's pocket. "We're going to take the summer to figure it out."

"She moves home tomorrow, right? Is she going to tell her family?" Riley came and joined him and Blake on the couch, perching on the arm. "They aren't shifter. They won't notice the pregnancy this early. She's so tiny, but I doubt she'll show 'til the fall."

"About that." Jasper winced. This was the part of his plan he needed his friends to be on board with. Because the males in their family *were* in fact shifter, and they'd notice the pregnancy instantly. "She and I, we're uh, moving back to Haxton for a few months."

Blake narrowed her eyes in disbelief. "What? Why?"

"Apparently, her parents are as religious as she made them sound out on the patio. She started rambling about them locking her in a basement when they found out. And she doesn't want to lie to them for months." Jasper sighed. "I told her she could live here for the summer and tell her parents she was doing some kind of bullshit mission work. She didn't love that idea since she'd be lying. Then my dumb ass mentioned that Maddi does that free medical clinic."

"She wants there to be some semblance of truth in her story." Blake nodded in understanding. "I get that. Lying to my parents isn't fun for me either." She leaned back against her mate when he started rubbing her shoulders. "I'm sure she could use the distraction."

"That's what she said." Jasper wrinkled his nose, bracing himself for what he was about to ask. "I need you guys to move home with us." They both opened their mouths to no doubt shoot down the idea, but he rushed to explain. "Just for a couple weeks, okay? The pack is going to notice she's pregnant the moment she steps into the house. I'm not ready for any of them to know it's mine. If we all go and we pass Callie off as Blake's friend who we're helping out, then it's a passable cover story."

"Look, Jasper, I like Callahan, I do. But I barely know her, and Jace isn't stupid. He's going to sense something is off with our story. Why can't you be honest with them about what's going on?"

"There are going to be questions I can't answer." Jasper shook his head. "You're the one who told me I needed to be patient and supportive, remember? You were right. I have to wait for Callie to decide what she wants to do, and until that happens, all the questions, all the opinions will make things harder on both of us." He glanced at his door at the top of the stairs. "If I wanted Callie stressed and scared, I'd let her move home to her crazy-ass parents."

Blake's expression softened, a small smile playing on her lips. "You *like* her."

"Of course, I like her." *What's not to like? She's beautiful and smart, and she needs me.* "I'm not in *love* with her, so get those silly hearts out of your eyes." He took her hands, ignoring Riley's low growl. "Will you help me? Please, doll, pretty please with Riley's dick on top."

Her smile grew and he knew he had her. "Fine."

"So the four of us are moving back in with Jace and Axie this summer?" Riley chuckled. "Who's going to break the news to Jace? Because it sure as hell isn't going to be me."

"It needs to be Blake."

Blake's jaw dropped. "Absolutely not. This is your, uh, situation, and Jace is your twin, who will no longer be able to walk around *his* house with his pecker hanging out. You make the call."

"Don't talk about Jace's dick please." Riley smiled down at his mate, sweet as sugar.

"Callahan is your friend in need, remember? Why would I call and let him know what's going on? I'm an uncaring asshole. If I act involved, then the story is going to unravel before we even get to Haxton. You need to call Axie and ask them if they are okay with it all. It's the only way that makes our story believable."

"You are a perpetual pain in my ass." Blake held up her hand, a stern expression on her face. "No comments about you *in* my ass or I back out of this charade."

Jasper mimed like he was locking his lips, but his first genuine smile all night made it difficult. He wasn't allowed to make innuendos anyway. He'd traded that right for Riley's pants the night Callie came over to study.

Blake huffed in annoyance as she plucked her phone off the coffee table. She hit Axie's name with more force than necessary, putting the call on speaker, wanting her reluctance to be on full display. The angry Barbie act was entirely comical.

"Lover. How's life with two yucky boys?"

Blake giggled at Axie's greeting. "It's gross. You know, except for all the mated orgasms and such. But that's not why I'm calling. I have a huge favor to ask of you and the evil mastermind who warms your bed."

"Okay, sure. What's up?"

"I was left no other choice than to make another female friend since you live three hours away, and my heart is perpetually aching for you." She licked her lips, cutting her gaze to Jasper. "And my new friend is knocked up."

"Oh wow. You fully enjoy jumping into drama, don't you?"

"You don't know the half of it." Her eyes narrowed, turning into a full-on Jasper glare. "She can't go home. Her parents would send her to some convent or something. Since we were talking about coming to visit for a few weeks anyway, I was wondering if she could come with. I thought she could help Maddi with her free clinic for a while, give her a safe space to figure out what to do next."

"Of course she can—"

"No." Jace's clipped voice cut through the line. "She can't come. In fact, all of you stay in Greenly. I just got my house back. I don't want it filled to the brim again. I rather enjoy fucking Axie wh—"

"If you want to keep fucking Axie at all, you're going to be a gracious host to this poor girl in her time of need." Blake, Riley, and

Jasper all hid soft laughter as best they could. Playing witness to Axie cutting off Jace at the knees was always a good time. "Do I make myself clear?" There was a short pause and possibly a mumble. "Louder for the people three hours away."

"Yes." They could all tell he was speaking through a clenched jaw. Jasper could picture his twin's posture clear as day: fists at his sides, eyes dark, but hella turned on by his mate's commanding attitude. "We'd love to immerse a human stranger into our daily shifter life, yet again. What could possibly go wrong?"

Axie ignored his reference to winter break when Riley and Jasper were fighting over Blake and breaking expensive shit in the house. "When are you leaving? Will you be here for pack dinner tomorrow?"

Fuck. Jasper forgot about dinner. When everyone was together, it was hard to hide their supernatural side. They weren't used to watching the way they spoke or acted, i.e., growling mates and supernatural abilities on full display. Their only saving grace would be that Callahan would most likely be too distracted by the pregnancy to pay much attention.

"Yeah, we'll be there," Blake answered for them. "If you wouldn't mind letting the pack know to not mention the pregnancy. She only found out this evening, but Riley sensed it a few days ago."

"I heard the flutter of a heartbeat tonight. Every male in our pack will be able to tell," Jasper spoke softly, hardly above a whisper, not wanting to let Axie know he was even part of this conversation. Hearing the baby's heartbeat, knowing it belonged to him…was heavy.

"Okay, sure. I'll warn them." Axie paused, the phone rustling like she was moving around. "Is the father involved at all? Is there anything else we can do to help her?"

Jasper's heart warmed at Axie's desire to help someone she'd never even met. She was a tough chick, sarcastic and wicked in all the best ways. She was kind though, so kind when it counted.

"The father is around. He uh, he has to go home for a few months, but he's agreed to help her no matter what direction she chooses. He's being a really good guy." Blake sent Jasper a small smile, letting him know that even though she was irritated to be part of his lie, she was still proud of the way he was handling things for Callahan. "Thanks for letting us bring her."

"No worries, glad we can help."

Jasper tuned out the rest of the conversation when it turned into more of their secret lover banter. Usually he'd join in, laughing and joking until their mates were so pissed and worked up they started growling and took away the phones.

He wasn't feeling it tonight though. His thoughts were upstairs with the sweet girl carrying his kid. He needed to go check on her. He needed to make sure she was truly resting.

Tomorrow would be a lot. Lying to her parents, lying to his pack. Digesting the truth of the pregnancy in the harsh light of day. He'd lied to her. He didn't think anything would be better in the morning. The dark made everything softer, more tolerable.

When the sun rose, he'd wake up with the stark, unyielding fact in the front of his mind.

No doubts, no maybes.

The baby was his, and its mother was now his responsibility.

Chapter Eighteen

Callahan

Callahan was awake, but she didn't want to open her eyes. If she opened them then it would all be real. She'd see Jasper's dark blue walls and white sheets. His framed family pictures, and dirty clothes shoved into a corner.

She could feel him against her back, his bare skin radiating heat. He showed more kindness and compassion last night than she thought he possessed. Supportive. Steady. Jasper was all the things she needed, and all the things she thought him incapable of being. Tears pricked the back of her closed eyelids, and she swallowed thickly, willing them away. What would they help anyway? They wouldn't wash away being pregnant. They wouldn't turn back time.

"I know you're awake, Callie."

Jasper's voice first thing in the morning was the sound women wrote songs about. Deep and rough. Its resonance seemed to travel over her body, leaving goose bumps in its wake. There was that old jerk *lust* again. Something that had never been an issue in her life until she met Jasper.

She wanted to pull the thick blue quilt over her head and hide away for the rest of time. Facing him in the light of day, after he'd had to hold her while she broke down, after he'd had to tuck her in. It was harder than it should be.

He'd seen her naked, but letting him see her vulnerable was too much.

"Come here." Jasper put his warm hand on her shoulder, his long fingers on her collarbone. He was so much bigger than her in every way. His height, his build, his personality. "I need to know you're okay."

She let him roll her over and into his arms. His body was like a radiator, the heat coming off him enough to melt glaciers. "I should go."

"You say that a lot when you're here." She felt him smile against the top of her head, making every hardened inch of her start to soften. "We need to get started packing up your dorm. We can grab some breakfast on the way. Are you hungry?" He winced as his gaze cut to his bathroom door. "My sister Maddi had to puke every morning before she ate for the first like four months of her pregnancy."

Pregnancy. That word coming from his young, gorgeous lips was surreal. She was pregnant. He'd gotten her pregnant. He'd heard her vomit and was worried she needed to do it again before he fed her breakfast and helped her pack up her life here.

"I know you want to do the right thing, and I can't tell you how much I appreciate it." She sat up, crossing her arms over her chest, her cheeks heating as she remembered him expertly removing her bra. "But you don't have to—"

"Callie. Stop." Jasper sat as well, the sheets sliding down his torso until his sculpted chest and abs were on full display. She fought the urge to lick her lips.

Jasper had told her he slept naked, always. She was thankful to discover he'd kept his briefs on last night. "I told you I'd help you, and I meant it. I meant everything I said last night." He reached out and put his hand on her stomach, making holding back those tears even harder. "We did this. You and me. And we are going to see it through, no matter what you choose. So stop saying you should go. Stop trying to let me off the hook like a martyr."

She nodded. Her smile weak as she wiped the moisture from under her eyes.

***

Packing the rest of her belongings hadn't taken much time. Her dorm room was small, and she shared it with a girl she'd never really taken the time to connect with. Her roommate had moved out as soon as she'd finished her last final, throwing a "see you next semester" over her shoulder on her way out.

Jasper divided her clothes into two separate suitcases. One she'd take with her to Haxton, and one she'd leave stored at Jasper's house until they got back. He told her he talked to his family last night and gotten everything squared away. He said they told everyone she was a friend of Blake's to take the weight of the family's pressure off, and that his sister Maddi was excited to have the help at the clinic.

Having a plan made her feel marginally better. One foot in front of the other. One day at a time. She knew she needed to figure out what to do about the baby, but it wasn't going to come to her overnight. She needed time to think of all possible outcomes, time to decide what would be best for them and the baby. *The baby.* She put her hand on her stomach, and for the first time, noticing how hard it was. It was like overnight abs.

"You okay?" Jasper's eyes moved to her hand, then back to meet her gaze. "You feel okay?"

She nodded. "Yeah." She was embarrassed she kept touching her stomach today, and that he kept catching her do it. "Nerves." She sighed, dropping her hand to her side, her fingers brushing her thigh where her shorts stopped.

Her father hated those shorts, he said they were too trashy, showed too much skin. Ugh. Her father. "I need to call my parents." She'd been dreading this moment from the moment Jasper had told her the test was positive. Speaking to her dad, hearing his voice, and lying to him... If Jasper was larger than life, her dad was his own galaxy and he demanded everyone rotate in the particular orbit he assigned. His expectations were higher than high, and his morals were etched in granite.

"Do you want me to wait in the hall? I can go load the truck, give you some privacy." He picked up two boxes in one hand and then used the other to sling her duffle over her shoulder.

Her breath left her in an audible sigh. He was perfection, his t-shirt stretched tight around his biceps, his muscles working overtime to help her.

Was there anything more appealing? Were these observations no more than pregnancy hormones? She couldn't remember ever feeling so physically attracted to another human in her life.

This wasn't her. This drooling, wanton mess.

"Uh, yes, um sure. That would be good, thank you." She grabbed her phone from her now-empty desk, smashing it in between her palms and twisting them nervously.

Jasper crossed her room in three strides, using his foot to pull the door all the way open. "I'll be right outside if you need me, okay?" He waited for her to nod. "Callahan, this has nothing to do with them, remember that. We can handle this. We've got this. They don't get to tell us what to choose."

She nodded again, her stomach turning over with worry and guilt.

She waited for him to step into the hall, his parting words giving her the strength and push she needed to make the call.

"Good morning, Callahan."

Her worry turned to actual dread at the sound of her father's stern voice. Her momentary strength entirely fleeting, like a hummingbird darting away so fast you almost missed it. "Morning, Dad."

"Are you all packed? I have some things to do at the office, but I should be in Greenly by five."

She took a deep breath, steeling herself, filling her lungs to capacity. "Actually, I was calling to see how you felt about a mission opportunity I was given yesterday." She covered half the phone, letting out that big breath.

"Mission?"

Mission. A beautiful word to parents like hers. Serving others while preaching about the lord: the perfect activity for a young girl. Heaven forbid she help others simply to help, no attempt at conversion necessary. "Yes. A friend of mine, Blake—"

"A boy?"

She closed her eyes, shaking her head at the instant thread of disdain in his tone. He said *boy* like it was a curse word. "No, Blake is a girl." She licked her lips, hoping she could sell this the way she needed to. "Her family puts on a free health clinic for kids during the summer. She's invited me to come and help for a month or so. I would love the opportunity, of course, but I wanted to see what you thought."

In order to get her father to agree to anything that wasn't his idea, she had to approach it carefully. Slipping it in from the side in a way that made him feel fully in control of the situation and her life. She and her mother were living in the universe he'd created for them and his parishioners. She wasn't deceitful; she'd simply learned how to survive as her father's child.

"Where will you stay? How long?"

At least he didn't ask if Blake's parents would be there to make sure she went to bed at the correct time. Her father's leash was short.

"I'll stay with her family, and it's for the whole summer. They've offered to store my things for me. I can ride home with her today. The clinic starts on Monday. She's from Haxton. A small town."

"I know Haxton." He paused. "There's a boys' school there."

Was he worried she'd spend the summer getting into trouble with high school boys? If only he knew of the lust-filled thoughts she was currently having about a boy who was becoming a man before her eyes.

She stepped to her window, peeking between the blinds to watch Jasper rearrange her stuff in the bed of his truck. He leapt up on the tailgate in one smooth motion, those biceps pushing at the confinement of his sleeves.

"Callahan, are you listening to me?"

"Yes, sir." She stepped away, letting the blinds audibly snap back into place. "There is a boys' school there, but they're out for the summer, of course."

"Your mother will be disappointed she won't see you. She's been looking forward to you coming home." Her father's tone softened when he mentioned her mother. He loved her, that was clear as day. He was a better husband than he was a father. It was almost like he wasn't quite sure what to do with a daughter. "It sounds like a great opportunity though, a great way to spend your free months."

"You think so?" This was the key to dealing with her father. This was the pivotal moment where she turned it around to make it sound like his idea. "I don't know though. I do miss Mom and—"

"No, Callahan. There is no better way to spend your free time than serving others and spreading the word of Christ. You have a whole summer off, and idle hands are the devil's workshop, you know that." He paused again, the sound of papers shuffling coming across the line. "You need to do this. I insist." She couldn't help rolling her eyes at how predictable he was. "I'll make sure there is enough money in your account to get you through the summer. Your mother and I will come visit as soon as you get back to Greenly."

They said their good-byes and she had all her tears wiped away by the time Jasper stepped back into her tiny empty dorm room.

Their lies were in order. Each family fooled into thinking something that wasn't entirely true. Guilt gnawed at her gut, but their deceit was necessary.

She didn't know how she felt about the pregnancy, and she didn't know how to handle the way she felt about Jasper.

Callahan had never felt so unsettled before, and the tears kept threatening to fall.

Chapter Nineteen

Jasper

They took two separate cars to Haxton, Riley and Blake in one, and Jasper driving Callahan in his truck. Jasper wanted the option to leave any time they needed. He wasn't sure how this would go, how Callahan would handle any of it. His family, his pack, it was large and growing all the time. It was hard to curb the otherworldliness of it all, which had been blaringly evident when Riley was forced to bring Blake into the fold a few months ago.

Jasper wanted to be able to whisk Callahan away, take her back to his place in Greenly where it would only be the two of them. The two of them and the tiny baby she wasn't sure she wanted to raise.

Did he want to be a dad? He knew he fathered the baby, and that knowledge would be with him every day, whether they chose adoption or anything else.

Being a dad was more than biology though. Did he want to be the one who was up all night? The one who took the kid to the doctor and taught him how to throw a wicked curveball? *Fuck.* He had no clue.

He'd lived a life wilder than most. Hell, he'd shot and killed his own old man. Still. At the core of it all, he was a nineteen-year-old kid with apparently too much testosterone for anyone's good.

When they'd stopped for gas, he leaned against his truck and asked, "You feeling okay? Carsick?" He found it was much easier to focus on Callahan in the present than it was to think about their future together.

She stood crunching on the crackers he'd bought in the mini-mart. Once, Maddi threw up in Linc's lap on a road trip. Jasper wanted Callahan to avoid doing that if at all possible.

"I feel okay, the crackers help, thank you." He noticed her putting her hand to her stomach, something she'd been doing more and more often.

"Can you tell? Do you feel any different? Aside from the puking, I mean." He wanted to touch her stomach too, to see if he could tell the baby was causing even more changes to the petite redhead's body other than her expanding boobs, at which he paid way too much attention.

"It's hard, like rock hard." She laughed lightly, a sound he hadn't heard since their ill-fated night together. "I think my abs might be harder than yours right now."

He patted his own stomach. "No one's abs are harder than mine."

"Oh yeah?" She reached over and took his hand, pulling it across her body and placing his palm on her skin. She was warm. He swallowed past the new ever-present lump in his throat. Her stomach *was* hard, like stone. He applied a little pressure, focusing on the faint sound of the baby's heartbeat. He rubbed his hand in a small circle, wanting in that moment to reassure them all.

"For what it's worth, I'm sorry." Reluctantly, he took back his hand. "I didn't, fuck, I didn't mean—"

"To get me pregnant?" She scoffed, showing him her profile as she looked across the gas station's parking lot. "I assumed you didn't do this on purpose, Jasper." She shrugged, her fingers knotting together at her waist. "We weren't careless."

No, that they weren't. In fact, he'd been more careful with her than he'd ever been. He'd gone slow, he'd made sure she was okay every step of the way. He let her stay the night, he'd pretty much demanded it. He wanted her to know she mattered, that her trust mattered to him. Look where that trust had gotten her though.

"We're going to get through this, Callie. We're all going to be okay. One way or another." He glanced over at her, smiling when she met his gaze. "I promise."

Her chin dropped to her chest, breaking their connection. "Well, for what it's worth, I won't hold you to that promise."

He wanted to protest. He wanted her to hold him accountable for every stupid word he ever uttered.

He wanted her to ask that he keep his promise, that he swoop in and take care of the three of them.

Jasper wanted someone in his life to require more from him. His twin was a force all on his own, taking the world in his capable hands and reshaping it to fit his demands.

Riley existed with Blake, breathing the same air, maintaining the same heartbeat. Maddi, Linc, and Allison were a family, a perfect unit that was thriving as were all the other mates.

Callahan was *his* responsibility. and she should want more from him.

"Will you tell me about your family? Please." Callahan put her hand back to her stomach. "I don't think I can take any more surprises at the moment. Don't leave anything out. I need to know what I'm walking into."

Well fuck him running. He sent up a silent prayer her next surprise wasn't Riley shifting in the damn dining room. "Uh, you know, we're your run-of-the-mill boarding school family formed out of loneliness and necessity."

That wasn't a total lie. He understood now Riley's desire to tell Blake as close to the truth as possible before she was able to see the whole picture. Jasper didn't want to lie to Callahan; it didn't sit right with him, turned his gut.

She wasn't his forever, but she was carrying his child, which could definitely account for his feelings.

"Jace is my twin. We met Riley our freshman year at St. Leasing. We were separated from our families, stuck in this small mountain town with no one but each other, you know? Baseball was life, so we spent the most time with our coaches."

He cleared his throat, wetting his lips before he continued to weave their tale into something that made sense to her human ears. "Eventually our coaches all got married and started popping out kids left and right. They brought us into the fold, and before we knew it, we were honorary big brothers celebrating every milestone together."

"Jace is engaged to Axie?"

He nodded, keeping his eyes on his feet, avoiding the setting sun. "Yeah, engaged and living together. Blake and Riley you already know. Then there's Linc, Maddi, and Allison. They're the ones I'm closest with.

"Keller and Molly have twin boys, Bhodi and Riot, Dom and Corey have Hadley, who Riley calls his little sister. Then Pen and Baze have Oliver."

Jasper couldn't help his gaze as it slid to Callahan's stomach. Would their baby join the pack? They weren't mated. If Callahan decided to keep it, they'd be co-parenting. Which meant joint custody and two separate homes. At most, their baby would spend every other week with him, and maybe school breaks and summer months with his cousins.

They stood in silence again for a few moments. He missed his pack, but he was nervous to see them. Scared they'd take one look at Callahan and know the tiny heartbeat inside her belong to him.

"They won't know that you're the father."

She said those words like a statement, but he couldn't help but hear a question in her soft tone as she seemed to pull his thoughts right out of his brain.

"Callie, I uh, I want you to be able to make up your mind all on your own, okay? I don't want my family giving their opinion or trying to sway you in any way." He reached over, putting his hand on her arm. "This isn't me being an asshole or a coward. This is me wanting to give you want you need."

"What if what I need is for you to tell me what I should do?" Her voice was getting quieter with every word she uttered, slowly breaking his heart and stealing the air from his lungs.

"Is that really what you want? Me to make this decision for all of us?" He'd do it if that was what she actually wanted. He'd hole himself inside his twin's mountain mansion and wrack his brain day and night. Weigh the pros and cons, ask his brother his opinion, drink and consult with his best friend. He'd do it if she asked him to.

"No." She sighed, the sound once again coming out like it was painful. "But I would like to know what you want to do. You said it was my choice." She put her hand on her stomach. "This affects both of us though, doesn't it?"

That was the million-dollar question.

What did he want to do?

He wanted *to do right* by Callahan. And if she didn't choose the abortion option, then he also needed to do right by that baby they never meant to make.

He wanted to save them all; he wanted to have no regrets. He wanted to make the right choice. "Honestly, I don't know. I want our kid to have a good life, a great life. I have money, lots of it. I have support. I could raise our baby, and it would be wrapped in love and family and acceptance."

"But?"

"But." He licked his lips, glancing her way to catch her bottom lip trembling. "We're so fucking young. Your parents don't seem like they'd ever be on board with being grandparents under these circumstances, and we barely know each other, Callie."

He couldn't give her his full answer because he couldn't give her the whole truth. She wasn't his forever. She wasn't his mate.

He liked her, he lusted after her, and then he'd fucked her.

That was where that was supposed to end.

He wasn't in love.

He wasn't growling at anyone who dared to get close to her.

He wasn't enamored.

His shifter wasn't clawing at his soul, demanding he claim the petite beauty standing next to him.

He'd made a mistake.

He'd tainted someone who was never meant to belong to him.

Chapter Twenty

Callahan

Callahan had Jasper tell her all about the people in his family, the people she would be meeting. As aspens gave way to pine, signaling they were getting closer and closer to the place and people he called home, she thought, she should've asked him more about where they were heading. Driving through the massive iron gates of his twin's house was surreal. It was like driving into an alternate universe where everything was big and imposing. The estate was huge, cut into the side of a mountain. There was fencing and cameras everywhere. Everything seemed to be totally high tech. She watched Jasper lean out his truck to an eye scanner to access the gate and then enter a long passcode to open the garage. Jasper parked his truck, shadowing them in darkness.

"What does your brother do for a living?" She wasn't sure the Pentagon would be any less secure.

"He's, um, in charge of stuff."

"In charge of stuff?" She blinked, her eyes trying to adjust. "That's vague."

Jasper stood at the back of his truck. "He has investments and companies, and he's just, I don't know, in charge of stuff and people." He waved his hand around, like he was knocking away his ambiguous answer and her wanting more clarity. "To be honest, I don't really know what he does all day."

He grabbed a few of their bags and hoisted them over this shoulder. Three bags, one shoulder and one rippling bicep.

She was overly invested in Jasper's arms and the way they worked. She'd never ogled someone before, but she couldn't seem to stop when it came to him.

Riley and Blake had inched in beside them a few minutes ago. Riley held all their bags as well, his hand resting on Blake's lower back. Those two were a really pretty couple. They were doing her and Jasper a favor, pretending to spearhead the summer mission project. She owed them a big thank you.

"Everyone is already here," Riley said.

All his attention was focused on Jasper, their eyes locked as if they were speaking silently. They interacted with a familiarity she'd never experienced. She'd never had a best friend like that, and seeing them together made her realize there was yet another thing she'd missed out on.

"You ready for this?" Riley smiled at her.

She wanted to say *nope*. She found out she was pregnant less than twenty-four hours ago. Now she was even farther from home and was about to meet a bunch of people for the first time while lying about why she was here and who she was.

She wasn't like this. She didn't have an interesting life full of drama and lies. She was Callahan. Straight-A student, ideal daughter, quiet bookworm.

She went to church twice a week until she moved away for college. Now she was in a strange place with a gorgeous guy who'd seen her all the way naked and done things to her body she didn't know were possible.

"Callie?"

"Hm?" She glanced at Jasper to find him staring at her with a sad smile on his lips. He'd looked at her that way often since she'd thrown up the banana concoction. It was as if he was apologizing every single chance he got. She needed to talk to him about that. She didn't need his pity or his sad smiles. "I'm sorry, did you say something?"

He stepped forward, putting his huge hand on her shoulder, his palm dwarfing her small body. "When we go inside, you need to stick with Blake. As far as anyone knows, she's the reason you're here. You and I? We only know each other through her. Got it?"

She nodded, letting him know she understood the way to play this. "Do they know I'm pregnant?"

"Axie and Jace do." Jasper's gaze cut to Riley, then back to her so quickly she almost missed it. "It's up to you if you want to announce it to everyone else."

"Do you?" she whispered, her stomach rolling with nerves as she peered up at Jasper.

Over the last two days, she'd experienced every emotion a person could have. But right now, she was nervous.

She was meeting Jasper's whole family.

It wasn't lost on her that if she and Jasper chose to parent this baby, these people would be in her life for the next eighteen years. At the very least. Jasper's family would be around her child when she wasn't. This would be where Jasper brought him or her for holidays and to play with cousins.

She wanted to make a good impression.

But more than that, she wanted to *like* these people.

"Callie." Jasper winced, his hand resting casually on the small of her back, like she'd watch Riley do with Blake. "I don't think it's a good idea for them to know I'm the father. Not yet anyway."

Meaning it was her decision *alone* whether she wanted to share the pregnancy news with anyone inside his brother's home.

So far, Jasper had been right beside her every step of the way. Yet, she couldn't help the loneliness gathering inside her, spreading through her veins and into her heart. She was suddenly so tired, exhausted from all the choices she needed to make.

She nodded. "Let's not tell anyone else tonight." She didn't think she could handle much more of this day. She longed for a bed, and for sleep. For hours of nothingness. She needed a break. Her brain needed a break.

Blake reached down, taking her hand and giving it a playful squeeze. "Well, let's go introduce you to the circus these two dragged us into, huh?"

Callahan couldn't help but return Blake's grin, her good humor and mood. She was so full of light and mischief, it was contagious. Callahan let Blake pull her into the house, wincing when she called out loudly, "Lover, I'm home."

A gorgeous girl with long dark hair came bounding into the mudroom from what looked like the kitchen. She was wearing leather leggings and a crop top, her feet bare. She jumped up and down, clapping with a massive smile on her face.

"Oh, how I've missed—" She stopped short, her eyes narrowing and her plump lips pursed. She glared down at their still-joined hands. "Are you cheating on me?"

"Yes." Blake used her hold on Callahan to make her do a spin. "This is my *new* lover, Callahan. She's brilliant and kind. Not one wicked bone in her little body. She's everything you're not."

The woman Callahan assumed was Axie scoffed. "Well then, I'm left with no other choice." She stepped forward and engulfed both Blake and Callahan into a warm embrace. "We're now in a throuple." She laughed, her warmth and acceptance instantly putting Callahan at ease. She pulled back, beaming and utterly beautiful. "Anything you need, anything at all, just ask, okay?"

"Thank you." Callahan chewed on her lip for a minute, trying to get her emotions under control. "For, well, everything." If she listed all the ways these virtual strangers were helping her, they'd miss dinner.

"Ah, if it isn't my second and third favorite boys on the planet." Axie hugged Jasper and Riley while they good-naturedly argued about who was first and who was second. All of them were super close. They joked and laughed and seemed ecstatic to see each other.

The love between them was almost palpable.

Callahan was envious, and a pang hit her heart: she'd never belong like they did.

Jasper stood behind her, his hand moving down to her back where Axie couldn't see. He moved his lips closer to her ear, whispering softly, "I'm right here, okay? Even if it doesn't seem like I'm with you in this, I am." With those words he stepped past her and disappeared from sight. She was alone with Blake and Axie, the two of them staring at her like she might implode at any moment.

"You ready?" Blake asked.

Callahan nodded and followed them through the kitchen and around a corner to a room filled with a massive dining table. It was the largest piece of furniture she'd ever seen. It belonged in a medieval castle, not this modern mountain marvel she was standing in.

Axie wrapped her arm around her shoulders and Blake was holding her hand. They were letting her borrow their solidarity, and she was grateful. "Family, this is Callahan. She's gorgeous, I know, don't stare at her though."

Blake pulled Callahan down the table, pointing at people and throwing out names at a rapid-fire rate. "Dom, Corey, Hadley, Linc, Maddi, Allison, Baze, Pen, Oliver, Keller, Molly, Bhodi, Riot, and that's Jace. He's Jasper's twin. They may look alike, but Jace is smarter and meaner."

"Uh, it's nice to meet everyone." Callahan wasn't sure what else to say. She met Jace's gaze across the table. "Thank you for letting me stay. You have a beautiful home."

Jace sent her a small smile and inclined his head. "No thanks necessary. We're happy to have you." He and Jasper did look alike. They had the same hair color, the same eye color, and the same strong jaw. She could tell though, even from one interaction, that was where their similarities ended.

Suddenly everyone was eating and speaking all at once. It was carefully controlled chaos and she wasn't sure how anyone knew who was saying what. There was laughter and baby giggles, mashed potatoes smashed in tiny fists.

A lady sitting next to a blond guy spoke up. "Callahan, I can't tell you how grateful I am for the help this summer." *Grateful for the help,* that must make her Maddi, and the man beside her, Linc.

"There's only one doctor in Haxton, and getting most of these physicals out of the way takes a huge load off her shoulders." Linc, Maddi's husband, made a weird sound in his throat, as if he was choking.

She whacked him harshly on the back, smiling sweetly. "Chew your food, dear."

"Honestly, I'm happy to help." Callahan returned her smile, trying to put some enthusiasm in her tone when she really wanted to go take a nap. "If it wasn't for this opportunity, I'd be working for my father all summer, and having already spent four summers doing that, I'm sure I'll have a much better experience with you." She meant her comment as a joke, but she could see Jasper's frown from across the table. His opinion of her father, her parents, was low.

Riley took a baby from the lap of her mother, placing her on his knee and seamlessly feeding her and himself. Callahan tried not to stare.

"So, Callahan." Jace neatly wiped his mouth before continuing. "How did you and Blake become so close?" Jasper's twin glanced from her to Blake, then to Riley, a smirk on his lips. "I figured Riley wouldn't really be into *sharing* his girl anymore." Axie reached over and put her hand on top of his, her nails obviously digging into his skin.

Callahan let her gaze drift around the table; all eyes were on her. She liked Jasper's family, she did. They were entertaining and kind. But being the center of attention wasn't her favorite place to be. "We met in our English lit class."

Jace nodded, taking a sip of his wine before continuing. "Jasper, weren't you in that class with Blake as well?"

Jasper chuckled, his hand wrapped around a frosty cold beer glass. "Yeah, when I decided to show up to class, I was. There were plenty of days when I had better things to do." He winked.

She couldn't help her frown. Jasper never missed a day of class; why was he acting like he barely attended? She guessed he was playing a part, playing into the player persona of his. Was that for her sake? To make sure there wasn't a connection between them? Or was this the part he always played for his family?

"You pulled a high B in English lit. How'd you manage that without showing up?" Jace was studying him over the top of his wineglass again, his eyes assessing his brother like he was searching for something.

Blake had mentioned that Jace was smarter, maybe she meant more analytical.

"Luck." Jasper grinned, draining his beer and wiping his mouth with the back of his hand. Jace let it go, humming in response. "Why are my grades being sent to you in the first place?"

"They aren't. He hacked the system." Riley popped a piece of steak into his mouth, chewing politely. "I'm assuming."

Jace nodded with a small shrug, like hacking into the university's computer system was no big deal.

The table got quiet for the first time since they sat down. The clatter of a fork as it hit a porcelain plate was loud and disruptive. The dark haired tattooed and pierced man sitting across from her and next to Jasper gasped, a shocked expression on his face. He stared at her, eyes narrowed, then he shifted his gaze to her right where Blake sat. "Riley, Blake, is there something you two want to tell us?"

"Nope." Riley grinned from his place next to his girlfriend. "There surely is *not*. And maybe you should read through the group text before you show up to family dinner, yeah?"

"I hate the group text. I have it silenced on my phone." He was balancing Oliver, their baby boy, on his lap.

Callahan hadn't been able to stop watching him, or any of the other babies. Would they have a boy? Would she be holding him throughout a big family dinner? Did she want to be? In an ideal world, yeah, she did. She wanted to have money and support. She wanted to have everything she needed to provide her baby with a great life.

Her stomach clenched with the truth. It was the first time she'd admitted it to herself.

The tattooed man's wife raised her hand in the air. "That's my bad. I should've relayed the message."

What message? She wanted to ask, but she assumed it was most likely none of her business. She wasn't part of this large, loud, chaotic family, and chances were, she never would be. Her child could be though. There were babies scattered in laps all over the place, and these were the children her baby could grow up with.

"Jasper, take your sister. She keeps trying to crawl out of my arms to get to you anyway." Maddi passed the baby across the table, holding her high in the air until Jasper grabbed her. He blew a raspberry on her round belly before settling her onto his lap.

Callahan couldn't look away. Jasper with a sweet baby, smiling down at her as he fed her small pieces of steamed broccoli. He was a natural, and it was incredibly sexy.

There was that word again. The one she couldn't help thinking when it came to the guy who'd knocked her up.

Jasper's gaze darted up to meet hers, almost like he'd been able to feel her attention on him. His smile was small, kind. He knew what she was seeing, what she was thinking. There was no way he didn't.

"I'm pregnant." She spoke the words softly, yet all conversation stopped again. "My family doesn't know, and I, uh, well, you guys are all so nice. I didn't want to lie to you all summer."

Blake pulled her in for a hug and Axie winked at her from across the table.

Callahan refused to meet Jasper's gaze.

She was too afraid of what she would find.

Chapter Twenty-One

Jasper

Callahan was sitting by Blake, talking with Axie, the two of them bringing her into the fold of their friendship. It warmed his heart seeing his family take to Callie like that. He knew telling them about the pregnancy was hard for her to do. He hated that she was alone. He hated he didn't reach across the table and take her hand, telling his pack that he was the father. He knew in the long run things would be easier on Callahan this way, but he loathed himself at the moment. As soon as they decided what they were going to do with their future, he'd tell everyone the truth. He made a silent vow, trying to ease the odd ache in his chest.

Jasper glanced up, pulling his attention away from Allison to gauge how his pack was reacting to the news. Baze knew, he'd heard the baby as soon as there was a lull in conversation, although he'd assumed it was Riley and Blake who were expecting. Thank god, he hadn't pushed for answers and instead had taken his cell out of his pocket and covertly read through all the missed text messages he habitually ignored.

Jasper could feel his twin's glare on the side of his face, the heat from his pack beta's gaze almost searing with intensity. He turned to meet his gaze, trying his best to hold strong. Jace had already figured out Jasper had to know Callahan. They'd shared a class, and she was supposedly one of his roommate's new best friends.

He sighed, his gaze moving to his lap. Jace was powerful, and pack dynamics demanded he submit when Jace willed it.

"Dammit, Jasper." Jace cursed so low Jasper was pretty sure he was the only shifter at the table who could hear him since they were seated so close.

Jasper kept his gaze in his lap, not wanting to see the disappointment in his twin's face. He'd been stupid to think Jace wouldn't figure it out. It was one of his best skill sets: seeing the problems coming, putting clues together to keep them all safe. Of course, he flushed it out. Of course, he knew that Jasper was the baby's father.

"Have the three of you been having a good time in Greenly?" Corey was feeding Hadley and herself at the same time, never missing a beat. The pack was moving past the pregnancy announcement, taking pity on Callahan by removing the scrutiny from her.

"Living with two boys isn't as annoying as I assumed it would be." Blake grinned, scraping mashed potatoes off her fork.

"Out of the three of us, you're hands down the messiest." Jasper didn't feel at all like joking around, but he had a part to play. Jace may have things all figured out, but the rest of the pack was still in the dark, and that was where they needed to remain. So joke he would. "I found half of a Hot Pocket in the couch last week."

Blake rolled her eyes but didn't deny it belonged to her.

"Still, I'm sure it was a bit of a shock to the system." Corey glared at him from her spot on the other side of the table. Linc and Maddi never cared about his player ways; they'd both been the same as him before they met and fell in love. Corey, however, was the mother hen. He was sure she'd been relieved when Riley bonded with Blake and she didn't have to worry about her precious *buddy* continuing to follow Jasper's fuck-boy lead. "Can't be fun bearing witness to Jasper's never-ending parade of one-night stands."

For fuck's sake. Jasper couldn't help but glance up at Callahan. Her nose was wrinkled, like she smelled something she didn't like.

He assumed it was more like she *heard* something that turned her stomach. The girl pregnant with his baby didn't need to be reminded of how many had literally come before her.

Her palm went to her mouth, and she stood abruptly. He couldn't help himself. He didn't seem to have control over his limbs. He jumped to his feet as his chair crashed to the floor. "Second door on the right." He pointed out of the dining room, showing her in which direction she could find a toilet to puke.

She bolted. And he made himself sit back down even though all he wanted to do was go help her. He was the reason she was going to be loudly vomiting in mere seconds. They were shifters, most of them would be able to hear it all too clearly. His wolf preverbally picked his head up, alerted to Callie's distress, and now to the fact that they were home with their pack.

"Quick reflexes, bro." Linc nodded, like he was impressed.

Jasper swallowed thickly, adjusting Allison back to his lap. "I was in direct firing line." He shrugged it off like it was no big deal.

"Uh, Blake?" Molly leaned forward. "Aren't you going to go help her?"

She made a face, wincing. "Ew, no way, I hate… Dammit." Blake clenched her teeth, smiling tightly while secretly shooting Jasper a death glare. "Of course, I'm going to help *my friend*." She made a show of wiping her mouth and setting her napkin in her chair. "Why wouldn't I go hold her hair back while she pukes her guts up?" She was still muttering her annoyance as she strode out of the dining room.

"Blake is going to pay you back for that." Jace leaned over and whispered next to his ear. "And I hope she makes it hurt like hell, you irresponsible prick."

"Jasper, make yourself useful and help me grab dessert." Axie stood from her spot to Jace's left, gathering her dinner plate as well as the empty ones nearest to her. He handed Allison across the table to Linc and piled plates in his palm before following his twin's mate into the kitchen. "Duck out and go help Callahan."

"You know?" He shouldn't be surprised, if Jace figured it out, Axie could too.

"Jace may have been whispering, but I learned a long time ago to read his moods, whims, and lips." She put her hands on his shoulders, shaking him lightly. "We're going to figure this out, okay? But right now, go take over for Blake. My lover shouldn't have to clean up your messes, no matter how many Hot Pockets you find in the couch."

He gathered what he needed, what he already knew would help Callahan. It felt right being beside her while she was going through all this. Like he was paying penance. A penance he deserved and didn't mind, at the same time.

Blake was standing outside the door. "She wouldn't let me in, she said no one wants to watch someone vomit." Blake gave him a quick peck on his cheek. "But that doesn't mean she doesn't need help."

He didn't bother to knock, or to ask.

After Blake headed in the direction of the kitchen to hide out without him having to ask, he pushed the door open. "I brought you some water and crackers." He set his offering on the edge of the powder room sink, then sank down onto the cool tile beside Callahan. "I'm sorry my level of fuck-boy made you puke."

She snorted, which was unlike her. "Are you referring to the one-night stand parade I was part of, or the baby you left in my womb?"

"Both, I guess." A single evening with Blake and Axie as bookends, and already sweet, polite Callahan was making sarcastic comments like the best of them. Not that he didn't earn it.

"It's okay. It wasn't the reminder you've slept with most of the freshman and sophomore class at UNC. It was the cheesy broccoli." She took the water bottle he'd opened for her, swallowing a small sip. "I don't think the baby likes cheese." She'd been repulsed at the smell of the pizza the other night as well, so that made sense.

"I thought you didn't want to tell them you were pregnant. What made you change your mind?" A heads-up would've been nice. Her softly spoken admission almost made *him* vomit all over the dinner table.

She shrugged, taking another drink of water. "They were all being so nice, so inviting and kind. If we do decide to co-parent, I don't want their first memories of me to be deceit."

"No one would blame you for not wanting to announce your pregnancy to a room full of strangers." He understood her need for honesty and how much lying bothered her. He also knew that no matter what, no one in his pack, his family, would ever think unkindly about the mother of his child.

She used the corner of the sink to pull herself up, putting the lid back on her water bottle. "I'm really tired. Do you think you can show me to my room?"

"Jace, my twin, he knows the baby is mine. He put two and two together when you mentioned the English lit class."

"Oh, I'm sorry. I wasn't even thinking and—"

"No." He stood, resting his hand on her shoulder, his fingers engulfing her chest and collarbone. "Don't apologize. There's nothing to be sorry for. None of this is your fault. I wanted you to know that once everyone leaves, if you want me to lie down with you, uh…I can."

He didn't like the thought of her being alone, being sad and scared in a room she'd never set eyes on before. The house, the people he'd surrounded her with, they were all foreign and he couldn't image how unnerving all this was for her.

"I'm okay." She pulled her bottom lip between her teeth. "I don't think it's a good idea, for, um, well, me to depend on you, you know? We aren't together, and we don't know what we want to do about the pregnancy, and… I appreciate how wonderful you were last night, but I'll be okay."

"Is there anything else I can do? Anything I can do to help you make your decision, to make this easier on you?" He knew she was overwhelmed because he was too.

She licked her lips, turning to him slightly. "It would help to know what you want to do. I know you said it's my choice and I appreciate that, I do. But it would make my decision easier if I knew what your choice would be. If it was up to you."

The one thing he couldn't give. He'd been wracking his brain since Riley told him about the pregnancy, trying to figure out how he felt and what he wanted for the three of them.

The thought of someone else raising his shifter son didn't sit right. He wouldn't be able to make sure his first shift went well, or whether he was learning everything he needed to about their culture: about what it meant to have the soul of a wolf lurking inside them.

If it was a girl, man, that was almost worse. Could they guarantee she would never end up nineteen and pregnant by a complete loser like himself?

But raising a child, starting a family at his age, parenting with a woman who wasn't meant to be his? He wasn't sure he could do that either.

"Callie, I, uh, I think I need some more time, you know? I promise I'm trying to organize my thoughts, that I'm really thinking about this from all angles. I know I seem like a class clown, but I swear—"

"You aren't a class clown." She shrugged her small shoulders. "You're bright, and you try. The class clown seems like a part you feel you still need to play."

He tried, sure. He tried real hard to get into her pants, and look where that had gotten them. Sitting on the floor in his twin's bathroom, feeding a girl who wasn't his mate crackers so she wouldn't puke again.

He didn't want to tell her his packmates were right. He was a class clown and he cared more about a good time than a degree.

Fun had screwed him.

Fun betrayed its master.

Fun could fuck right the hell off.

Chapter Twenty-Two

Jasper

After Callahan washed up, Jasper had led her to the room she'd be staying in while they were crashing with Jace and Axie. It was across the hall and to the right, her door almost lining up between his and Riley's. He wanted her close, but he didn't want her to feel like she didn't have her own space. Time, space, patience, kindness. Those were all the things Blake had mentioned. Those were all the things he was striving to provide. Yet, it seemed like what she really needed was his opinion, his decision.

After the rest of the pack left, Jasper was on the couch with a glass of whiskey in his hand and his feet propped on the coffee table the way Jace hated. His twin pushed his feet to the ground before joining him. Axie coming over to perch on her mate's knee. "Have you two talked? Have you decided what to do?"

"No." Jasper's head fell back on the cushions. "She asked me what I wanted to do about the baby, after vomiting up her dinner. I don't have any answers for her. I wish like hell I did."

Axie hummed low, her finger tapping against her chin. "We could adopt the baby. Jace and I." She spoke those words like they weren't a huge deal, like they didn't change lives and rock Jasper to his core.

Jace jerked back, like his mate had slapped him across the face. "What?"

"If it's a boy, he will need a shifter family, right? We're just as young as they are, but we're settled. We're here with the pack and surrounded by kids and family. I want my own biological children one day, sure. But we could do this for her, for us, for that baby."

That baby? That was *his* baby. He rubbed at his chest where an odd ache had started to grow. He could feel his wolf start to come alive, sluggish but there. He hadn't felt his wolf's influence much when he was in Greenly, but since the night Callahan confirmed her pregnancy, he'd been making more and more of an effort to be present. He was beginning to push his will against Jasper's heart, his lungs expanding with the magic inside him.

Jasper watched as Jace's initial shock softened into something that looked a hell of a lot like acceptance and excitement. "Are you serious? You want to do that?"

"I do, I really do." Axie smiled, taking her mate's hand with stars in her dark eyes. "You know, we could even keep Callahan here. Sort of take them both in. If she ends up not comfortable with adoption, then we could let her stay here for a while. She could take online classes next year and—"

"No." Their attention cut to Jasper, to the sharp words he'd thrown at them, and at the low growl coming from deep in his gut. He'd surprised himself with how strongly he hated the idea of Jace and Axie taking in his kid and its mother. They were his responsibility, his to care for. *His.*

"What the hell is wrong with you? She's scared. She doesn't know what to do. You don't seem to have any answers either." Jace gestured to him with a wave of his hand. "You just said so yourself, seconds ago."

"I. Said. *No.*" He was breathless, raging at the notion his brother and mate would raise his child. In theory, he told Callie he'd help her pick a family if that was what she wanted to do, but now that someone was standing in front of him, wanting to raise his kid and set up its mother? Hell to the actual fucking no. Whether it was his pack or not.

Jace narrowed his eyes on his twin, seeing too much, always seeing more than the rest. "And there is your answer. You ridiculous asshat." Axie grinned from her seat on his knee, satisfaction swimming in her wicked smile. "All we had to do was give you an out. I knew you would never take it."

"Are you fucking kidding me right now?" His jaw was sore from how hard he'd clenched it, his hands still fisted at his sides, like he was preparing for a fight.

"Nope." Axie popped the "P." "I am not *fucking kidding* you, Jasper." She leaned forward, putting her hands on his shoulders, ignoring Jace's protest. "Scared, unsure, nervous, thrown for a damn loop? Of course. But from the moment she told the entire table she was pregnant and your fingers twitched like you wanted to reach for her, I knew what your choice would be."

He was pissed at them for tricking him, but he couldn't deny how good it felt to have that weight lifted from his shoulders. He knew how he felt, and as scary as it was, it was also a huge relief.

"She's everything I'll never be, and I fucked up her life. She deserved more than getting knocked up by a one-night stand." He sighed. "I'm not father material, but I'll do my best for that kid, if she'll let me."

"I give you a hard time, I know I do, but the truth is, you'll probably end up being the best dad in this pack. You love freely, you laugh and play and joke. But you protect the ones you care about too." Jace rubbed his hand on Axie's back. "You watch her. You watch her every move. You look at her stomach, your baby, constantly." Jace clinked his glass against Jasper's. "You three are going to be okay, bro."

"My wolf, he's protective over the baby, and he wants the baby, I think. He doesn't have many feelings about Callie, though."

He couldn't not say it. It was the truth and it sucked. Everything would be easier if she was his mate. They could fall in love, bond, and start their family. Age wouldn't matter. They would have everything they needed.

"She's not my forever."

"Not every family looks the same. We of all people know that to be true." Jace shrugged. "She's the mother of your kiddo, and that's enough for today, okay?"

Jasper nodded in agreement.

One day at a time.

Chapter Twenty-Three

Callahan

Callahan was lying in bed, trying to calm her nerves and her racing heart. She was in an unfamiliar house surround by virtual strangers. The one person she wanted to cling to, she knew she shouldn't. Her phone went off from somewhere inside her bag. She sat up, pulling her backpack closer to dig it out.

J: *You sure you don't want me to come lie with you for a bit?*

She did. She really and truly would've given anything to feel Jasper lying beside her. His scent and his heat always extinguished the chill in her bones. She was cold, and scared, and alone. She felt like a small child at her first sleepover. She wanted to call her mom and ask to be picked up.

She rested her hand on her stomach, the realization she was the mother now making her eyes prick with a new round of tears.

She chose not to answer him.

In the morning she'd tell him she fell asleep the moment her head hit the pillow. Her despair and confusion weren't his burden to bear. She knew he was going through his own emotional trauma, dealing with his own reaction to their new reality.

Jasper wasn't a bad guy. He wasn't careless and cruel and shallow. He was nothing like she'd originally thought.

He'd gifted her time and space, and now she was determined to allow him the same.

He didn't do this to her, he did this with her.

J: I can feel your sadness oozing through the walls, Callie. Stop acting like you're sleeping.

She read his message twice, unable to help the soft laugh that left her lips. It was utterly impossible. Her sadness wasn't traveling through the sheetrock to keep him awake. It was funny though. Even without knowing her, he knew her so well.

C: There's no way that's true. And I was moments away from a wonderfully peaceful sleep.

"Liar." Her attention flew to her open bedroom door. "I can see the track of tears on your face." Jasper was leaning against the doorframe backlit by the soft hallway light, his arms and ankles crossed, a knowing frown on his cute face.

"No one can see that well in the dark." She'd placed her phone on the nightstand the moment he called her a liar. She wasn't sure how long he'd been standing there, but she was sure her borrowed room was huge and it was impossible he could see clear across it in the dark.

He stepped farther into her space, peeling his shirt over his head in that innately sexy way guys had, and tossed it to the bench at the foot of her bed. "Let me lie with you until you're asleep. New houses are always scary on the first night." He lifted the covers, settling in beside her.

She took a deep inhale, trying to secretly fill her lungs with his spicy scent.

She appreciated him coming to check on her, she did. However, she refused to let it be more, let *him* be more. She needed to be able to take care of herself, especially if she ever wanted to entertain the idea of parenting their child.

For one more night though, she'd bask in what he was offering.

He snuggled under the covers, his warmth seeping into her very soul. She'd noticed that the first time she'd spent the night at his house. How hot he ran. How he slept without any covers, even with the fan on high. She held in her contented sigh at his nearness.

"I told you earlier I didn't have an answer for you, that I didn't know what I would choose if it was up to me." He cleared his throat, his arm pressed against hers from shoulder to wrist. "But I think I found my answer, if you still want to hear it."

She stopped breathing, her whole world standing still. She was equally terrified and curious. She'd asked him more than once what he wanted to do. After he told her though, there'd be no going back.

He couldn't unsay these next words, and she could never unhear them. Without his input though, she wasn't sure how she'd ever make up her mind.

He said he'd go along with whatever she wanted to do. What did he really want though?

"I would. I really would."

"I think I want to raise the baby together. Co-parenting and shit."

Co-parenting and shit. Definitely not the way she always pictured the conversation going with the father of her first child.

Yet, here Jasper was, wanting to give it a go. He'd make a good dad. She didn't doubt that. He was the opposite of hers for one thing. He was fun, and easygoing. He liked to laugh, and he liked for everyone around him to have a good time. He loved his family, that was obvious. Would he discipline their kid? Probably not. But she could be the structure, the stability. Jasper could be the heart, the warmth. Heck, he already was.

"Okay." *Okay.* What a lame thing to say after his admission. "I think, uh, I think I still need some time to figure things out. But thank you for telling me how you feel." She moved her hand a fraction of an inch, letting her fingers tangle with his for a brief moment. "It matters, Jasper, it matters a lot."

She wanted their child to have two loving parents and a big family. She wanted it to grow up at chaotic dinners like the one she'd sat through, listening to so many inside jokes her head seemed to spin.

They were in each other's business. They were loud and they loved. She'd never had that growing up, and if she was the only one raising their child, all it would have was her strict parents who didn't think laughter at the dinner table was appropriate.

"Yeah, well…" His words drifted off, like he'd lost track of what he was going to say.

"Well what?" She turned to face him, resting her cheek on her hand.

He mirrored her position, kicking off his covers as he moved. "I don't want you to feel alone, you know? In anything."

She couldn't help the small smile on her lips. "You're absolutely nothing like the guy I thought you were."

"Yes, I am." He shrugged one shoulder. "I am that guy, Callahan, I am. But luckily, we can be more than one thing."

"That's the dream though, right?" His brow furrowed like her comment confused him. "An overly confident playboy who is so good in bed you forget your own name who also happens to be a really kind man with a heart of gold." She wasn't sure what made her so bold, what made her say words she would normally be too shy and embarrassed to say. Maybe it was the spicy scent of Jasper filling her lungs like a drug.

He smirked, like she expected him to. "I made you forget your name, huh?"

Lips pursed, she nodded. "You did, but then you got me pregnant, so it's all pretty much null and void."

He snorted, making her giggle. "Callie, baby, did you just make a joke?"

She didn't answer him; instead she snuggled down under the covers and fell asleep to the feel of him smiling beside her.

Chapter Twenty-Four

Jasper

Callahan spent the next few days with Maddi, helping her set up the clinic in St. Leasing's trainer's office. They would start seeing patients next week, and they'd be busy for months. It wasn't only Haxton the free clinic served doing physicals for the athletes to be eligible to play during the next school year. Other small towns were included, and they'd flock to get in on the perk. Maddi would never turn away anyone who needed her help. She told Jasper that Callie was a hard worker, eager to learn and help any way she could.

He knew the truth though. She was begging for a distraction. Working herself until she was exhausted. She'd come home, eat, and then pass out. He hadn't spent much time with her, they'd barely spoken. But every night, after she'd climb wearily into bed, he'd join her.

Jasper wasn't irritated and clingy like Linc. He didn't care Callie was going to spend the summer surrounded by males dropping trou.

He didn't need to mark her, imprint his scent so fully that even humans would know to stay away. Instead, it was the thought of her feeling lonely, feeling hopeless or heartbroken that didn't sit right with him or his wolf. He couldn't stomach it.

She wasn't his mate. She couldn't be. He cared for her, sure. She was pregnant with his child, they'd always be close, they'd always have a deep connection.

He'd know if she was his forever.

Jasper had always reacted terribly to the pull of an unfinished bonding. First with Maddi, and then recently with Blake. It called to him, sent his wolf into hyperdrive. If Callie was meant to be his, the wolf lurking inside him would be losing his damn mind. Tearing at his insides to touch her, to claim her, to make her theirs irrevocably.

She was beautiful, there was no denying that. It was hard for him to keep his eyes to himself when she was around. He wanted to watch her, look for new signs of the pregnancy between them.

Everything about her drew him in, made him want her. The baby growing between them only heightened his longing. He felt so powerful, so male. He'd done that, he'd put that baby inside her. Fuck. He wanted to do it again. He would if he could, and it was such a stupid, silly feeling. It was almost embarrassing. When had his brain changed course from utter terror and regret to wanting to knock her up all over again?

"Why does she look like she's so much younger than the rest of us? We're all the same age." Axie tilted her head to the side, watching as Callahan braided her hair over her shoulder. They were all on the back patio, watching Callahan do some stretches outside in the sun.

Blake squinted, like she was looking for an answer to Axie's question. "She looks innocent. Like she's never gotten drunk and fallen off a table."

"Or done lines with strangers in a random bathroom." Axie wrinkled her nose, like the memory of when she met Riley and Jasper was unpleasant.

Jace sighed from his place by the grill. "Or killed anyone."

"It's like you knocked up an underage Sunday school teacher," Riley added to their little sidebar.

Jasper couldn't disagree. He'd definitely gotten the most innocent girl he'd ever hooked up with pregnant. He'd been drawn to her, Blake was right. He saw it now, albeit in hindsight. He'd wanted her in a way that wasn't natural. He didn't usually go for the sweet and inexperienced. They always ended up being a bit of a headache.

"Speaking of Sunday school, remember when she told us how her father is a pastor?" He scrubbed his hands down his face. "Not only was he the reason she wouldn't consider an abortion, she mentioned them locking her in a basement or sending her away to an aunt's house until she could give birth."

"Damn." Riley wrapped his arms around Blake's waist, drawing her into him. "They sound intense. When are you going to talk to them?"

"Uh, the twelfth of fucking never?" Jasper watched the mother of his child. "I was hoping we could forget they exist."

Blake scoffed. "Parents don't work that way."

"Mine did." Axie shrugged off the fact that her dad had essentially disowned her before she mated with Jace and moved into the mountain compound. She started ticking points off. "Pen is estranged from her parents. Corey's parents never come to Haxton, neither do Maddi's. And Molly just has her aunt, the retired one who's traveling the world."

"Okay, I take that back then, *my* parents don't work that way, and it doesn't sound like Callahan's are going to either." Blake rested her head back on Riley's chest. "If they're that strict and have that much control over her decisions, then I doubt they'll let her go without a fight."

"She's going to burn in the sun, she's already turning pink." Riley pointed out to the yard. "Us gingers, we gotta stick together."

Jasper swatted his hand away. "Stop looking at her." He turned, facing the rest of his family. "All of you stop looking at her." He shooed them away. Blake and Axie went inside to start making sides, the only food Jace would let them help with.

Today was Callahan's day off, and unlike the last two weekends, she hadn't spent her free time napping. Riley and Maddi assured him it was normal for her to be so tired. Today, though, she was awake and enjoying the backyard. It was warm, without a cloud in the sky.

The pack had decided on a barbeque, and no one made a dry rub quite like his twin. Who knew Jace's hidden talent would involve neurotically labeled spices and a food processor?

Jasper still hadn't told the rest of the pack what his connection to Callahan was. It wasn't that he was hiding it out of fear; he still wasn't ready for everyone's opinions and remarks.

Jasper licked his lips, tearing his eyes away from Callahan where she was lying in the sun. He turned, obstructing Riley's view of her in her swimsuit. It wasn't skimpy by any means; he wasn't sure Callahan even owned a bikini. Didn't mean he wanted everyone in his damn pack staring at her while she was exposed and unaware.

Riley narrowed his eyes, a smile playing on this mouth. "Are you blocking her from me?"

"She's not mine." Jasper was tired of telling them that over and over. "The baby is. It makes me protective." At least that was what he assumed was happening since blocking her from Riley had been a reflex, something his body and his wolf had wanted to do automatically.

"Sure, man, whatever." Riley gestured behind him to the patio where Jace was manning the grill. He said the meat needed to smoke for eight hours, so he'd woken them up at sunrise to help. "You want a beer?" Riley handed him a cold bottle, twisting the top once he took it in his hands. "We thought we'd go on a run after dinner. We haven't gone out as a full pack in months."

Jasper needed a run, that was for fucking sure. His skin felt too tight and his wolf was panting at the idea of busting free. The mountains behind his twin's compound were a playground to them. The rocky terrain and vast wildlife were like beacons to his shifter. He glanced over his shoulder, taking one more look at Callie before following Riley back to the grill and his twin.

"You get him to stop eye-fucking his girl? I was about to start taking bets on whether he'd come in his pants or get so frustrated he'd finally make a move."

Jasper growled at his brother, his jaw clenched so tight it ached up into his ears. "She's *not* my girl."

"I hate to point out the fucking obvious. But didn't we *just* go through this? Without the fetus of course." Riley crossed his arms over his chest. "You have been in Greenly, where we live as more human than shifter. You're away from the pack, your wolf is repressed, exactly like mine was."

Jace nodded, adding, "Remember what happened when Riley came home and started to shift and run with the pack? His wolf woke up and realized he'd shared his mate with his best friend and all hell broke loose."

Riley ticked off points on his fingers. "You banged her, you knocked her up, you brought her home to meet your pack, you've decided to live together for the summer, and you want to raise a kid with her." He snorted, his lips against his beer bottle. "She's yours, mate or not."

"My wolf woke up before we left Greenly, thank you very much." He didn't add that the fucker promptly went MIA again. "He was a smug bastard about the pregnancy, but that was as far as his intentions went."

Jace stepped to the edge of the wooden deck, peering across the yard at Callahan. Jasper was trying his best not to rip the eyes from his twin's head. He'd only prove their point all over again. "You only slept with her that once? And you used protection?"

He sat down in the nearest chair, exhausted by his entire existence at this point. "I mean, I banged her like four times that night, I'm pretty sure, but yes. I was careful, like I always am. I wore a condom and I pulled…" His words trailed off as images of them tangled in his sheets assaulted his memory. It was as if he was watching the two of them from the ceiling, seeing the way her creamy thighs stretched to cradle his body. Her red hair spread over his pillows, her nails scratching down his back leaving raised pink lines in their wake.

"You didn't, did you?" It was Riley asking, his voice an almost whisper.

"I, uh, I'm sure I did." He scrubbed his palms down his face. "I always do." He was promiscuous, but he was cautious to a fault. The last thing he ever wanted to happen was to accidentally get the wrong chick pregnant. He chuckled humorlessly to himself. "Fuck. I don't know, man. I honestly can't really remember now."

"Ask her," Jace urged.

"And I assumed I was the only high motherfucker on this patio." Jasper lost the war with his gaze, his attention back on Callahan as she held a book over her face. "Like I should say, 'Hey, Callie, no big deal, but do you remember if I pulled out during all the sex that created that baby you're growing?'" He snorted. "What would that help? What would it matter at this point?"

"I'm bringing this up, one time, and one time only." Riley sighed, cursing under his breath. "That night at the cabin with Blake, when we uh, shared—"

"How is Jasper not making disgusting crude remarks, that I'd kill him for, were I in your shoes?" Jace glanced between the two of them, shock written on his face.

"Oh, I can't," Jasper told his twin. "I traded Riley pants for a semester of no threesome jokes."

"Pants?" Jace cocked his head to the side. "What the hell are you three doing up there in Greenly?"

"It's a complicated balance." Jasper shrugged.

Riley continued. "Anyway, that night was the first time I was with her. It was also the first time I didn't pull out in my life. Like, I couldn't physically make myself leave her body. I wanted to fill her, even with the condom between us."

"Okay, so we're both fucking horndogs who have gone all caveman during a good time. That doesn't mean anything. At all." Jasper grabbed Callahan's discarded shorts from the chair under Jace's ass. "After that night it was so clear Blake was yours. You started acting insane. And once she got here? You both lost your minds." He pointed at the girl in question across the yard. "Callie has been here with me for a few weeks, and I'm still perfectly sane." He gestured wildly, accidentally smacking himself in the head with her shorts.

"Yeah, you seem real put together." Jace rolled his eyes.

"She's not having any symptoms either. No sign there's an incomplete bond." His shoulders dropped, all the fight and energy drained out of him. "I know you all wish she was mine, and honestly, so do I. It would make all this a hell of a lot easier." He left them there, stalking off across the yard to help Callahan get up and into the shade before her creamy skin turned any pinker.

Chapter Twenty-Five

Callahan

Callahan had never been so full in her life. Brisket, baked potatoes, beans, fresh homemade rolls, and more sweet tea than anyone should consume. She didn't like a lot of sugar normally, but since she'd gotten pregnant, she craved it at least once a day. After the barbeque all the guys had gone on a hike. She wanted to go too. She told Jasper she really needed to move and burn off some of what she shoveled into her mouth. He'd been weird, almost shifty while he convinced her to stay in the house with Axie and Blake. He said hiking up the mountain at night was dangerous when you didn't have the terrain memorized like they did.

Now she was curled up in bed, cozy after a long shower with three shower heads and an expensive face mask Axie had given her. This was how the other half lived she supposed.

She hadn't grown up poor, but her parents gave most of what they had back to the church. Decadence was a sin. And that shower was nothing if not decadent. She hadn't spoken to her parents other than to let them know she made it. She texted her mother a few pictures of the clinic, updating them as little as possible. She wasn't lying, she really was volunteering her time to help people who needed it. It wasn't a mission, and she wouldn't be spreading the gospel. Oh, and she was pregnant. But other than that, not lying.

She sighed, snuggling down deeper into her large comfy bed. Decadent. Lavish. The sheets felt amazing against her skin and the fluffy comforter had a bit of weight to it, which seemed to calm her. And everything smelled like Jasper. Every night she'd feel him slide in beside her. They didn't speak. It was simply the comfort of each other's presence. Two people, going through the same thing, being there trying to be the best they could be.

Jasper told her he wanted to raise the baby, to co-parent. She was leaning toward that decision too. Which meant telling her mom and dad: disappointing them while inviting their opinions and guilt-inducing glares.

She didn't have her own money, and she still had three years of school left. Would she need to quit and get a job? Where would they live? There was so much to discuss. She couldn't seem to make herself bring it up though. She was afraid. What if they disagreed? Would he walk?

"You're still up?" Jasper interrupted her thoughts, coming into her space and bringing that spicy scent with him. "Usually you're snoring by now." He glanced at his watch, a smirk on his lips.

She had more energy today than she'd had over the last couple of weeks or so. She'd had a short nap in the sun, which helped. She felt refreshed, more like herself. She was glad she was here in Haxton. Maddi was funny, smart, and didn't take anyone's crap. Callahan would learn a lot from Maddi, and from helping at the clinic.

"I don't snore." She scooted over, pulling the covers back and making room for him. "The baby snores, it just comes out through my nose."

Jasper kicked off his shoes, laughing. "I don't think it works like that. You need to take one of those biology classes Riley is insisting I pick up next semester." He settled in beside her, reaching to turn off the soft lamplight bathing the room in a golden glow. "Speaking of pregnancy stuff, we need to make you a doctor's appointment, huh?"

It'd been on her mind, and her to-do list. She got the name of the OBGYN all the ladies in Jasper's family used. "Yeah, Maddi sent me the information for her doctor."

Callahan wasn't necessarily putting it off, but she hadn't been ready. She knew seeing the baby, hearing the heartbeat, would make it all the more real. She could feel the changes happening inside her. The nausea, the sore breasts, the tightening of her stomach, the slight pull. She sighed, suddenly feeling a bit selfish. "I'm sure you're anxious to get the confirmation, right? I'm sorry, I didn't even think to—"

"No, it's not that. I know you're pregnant." He turned on his side, his hand reaching out to rest gently on her abdomen. "I saw the test. I've heard you vomit."

She mirrored his position, careful not to dislodge his touch. The heat from his hand, his scent, calmed her. When she was feeling queasy, a deep lungful of his sweatshirt or the feel of his palm on her helped. Not that she'd ever admit that out loud to anyone. "I'll call tomorrow and make an appointment."

"Can I come with you?" he whispered.

Jasper rarely whispered. He spoke like he knew exactly where he belonged in the world. Confident and in love with life. She envied that about him, and hearing him speak softly, almost like he was unsure of himself, upset her.

She put her hand on top of his. "Of course you can come." She tapped him with her fingers. "First step in co-parenting, huh? Doctor's appointments."

"Is that what we're doing? Is that what you've decided?"

Was that hope in his voice? She'd been busy helping Maddi, but what had Jasper been doing with his days? She knew he was working with his brother, and hitting the gym in the basement with Riley. She'd been so focused on herself, what she needed and trying to decide what she wanted, she forgot there were two souls waiting on her choices.

"Yeah. I think that's what I want." She shrugged, the large sleep shirt she wore slipping down to expose her skin. "That's what you want, right?" He'd told her that a couple weeks ago. Maybe he'd changed his mind since then.

He smiled, nodding. "That's what I want." His hand moved to her hip, shaking her playfully. "Co-parents and shit?"

"Co-parents and shit." She licked her lips, not sure why she felt so light in that moment. There was still a ton to figure out, logistics and cost. Her parents. Ugh, her parents. "I'll call Monday when I get a break and make an appointment."

"Let me." His grip on her tightened affectionally. "You two will be swamped, a line wrapped around the building. I'll call and make our appointment."

"Really?"

"Really. I went to most of Maddi's appointments, the receptionists there *love* me." He winked, looking cuter than he had any right to.

Her breath came out all shuddering and embarrassing. She prayed he didn't notice. Her pregnancy hormones were starting to make her a little, uh, hot. And bothered. Turned on. She refused to call herself horny, even in her own mind.

She closed her eyes and held her breath. She needed to rid her senses of the gorgeous, kind man warming her bed and begging to co-parent their child. She was smart. She knew she couldn't let herself feel anything but parent stuff for him, but she wasn't a dang saint.

Air rushed out of her lungs when she felt Jasper start to massage her hips.

"Roll over, let me put you to sleep." Gently, he guided her onto her other side. "Maddi's hips ached so bad the first trimester and the third." He began a slow methodical rhythm, squeezing and releasing. "When Linc worked late, I would rub her back." He snorted. "Don't tell him, he'll junk punch me on principle."

His fingers were magic, healing parts of her body she hadn't even realized were tense and hurting. "You two are close, you and Maddi."

"We are." He paused his movements and his words for no more than a few seconds. "Linc and I, we're a lot alike. Maddi saw that pretty quick. She took me in, the annoying little brother she never asked for." He chuckled. She was glad she was facing the wall and not staring into his pretty eyes while he worked her body so expertly. "They're my family."

"And you're lying to them." She was lying to her family as well, but she wasn't having to look into her mother's eyes every day while she did it. Jasper had gifted her with an out-of-sight-out-of-mind situation, and she was eternally grateful.

"I promised you time and space."

"And I had it." She grabbed his hand, placing it flat on her stomach. "We've decided. If you want to, we can tell the rest of your family."

"Yeah?" He pressed against her, pulling her back against his chest. "Maybe I can come meet you after clinic tomorrow? We could walk over to Linc and Maddi's, tell them after dinner."

He sounded more excited than she'd expected. They were nineteen and were accidentally having a baby. Not dating, not in love. Just pregnant.

She allowed herself one small moment of jealousy. Jasper was looking forward to telling people he was going to be a dad. He knew his family would support him no matter what. She longed for that level of comfort and certainty. That type of understanding.

She knew she was going to receive the exact opposite from her folks when the time came.

"Sure, if you're ready, then I'm ready too."

Instead of moving back to her side of the bed the way she knew she should, she allowed herself to snuggle deeper against Jasper.

She wanted to steal his emotions, his warmth, and his comfort.

She knew it was wrong to rely on him. It would only make the rest of her life colder. But she was too weary and too emotionally drained through and through.

She was out of strength for the day.

Tomorrow she'd be smarter, more independent.

Yeah, tomorrow she wouldn't even let him sleep in here with her.

Tomorrow.

Chapter Twenty-Six

Jasper

Jasper threw open the double doors wide, walking the familiar halls in the direction of the trainer's clinic. He'd spent more time here than he'd spent anywhere else. The coach's offices for game strategy and pack discussions. The weight room and the locker rooms. Hell, he'd snuck dozens of girls into the showers after games. All the public school chicks wanted to see the inside of their hallowed private halls. It'd been as easy as taking candy from a baby. Eww. Wait. He was going to have a baby. What if it wasn't a boy? What if he had an innocent, perfect daughter? Would some disgusting fuck-boy try to talk her into the shower?

"Hey, what are you doing here?" Maddi wrinkled her nose, hands on her hip. "You aren't meeting some poor girl up here, are you?" She glanced behind him. "I thought Dom told you not to do that anymore."

He was, in fact, meeting some poor girl here. The beautiful, innocent angel he'd knocked up. He wanted to tell Maddi and Linc together though. "I came to see you, Nurse Maddi. Wanna cup my balls?"

She popped him upside the head but laughed at his joke anyway. "We're done for the day, but come to the house. Linc is in charge of dinner while I'm working the clinic, so it should be interesting and most likely inedible." She threw her arm around his shoulders and steered him to the door.

"Do we need to wait for Callie? Or did she already head out?" He hoped like hell he didn't sound overly interested. He was though. Was Maddi really about to leave his pregnant, uh, *friend* here by herself? In an empty school where horny assholes have been fantasizing about her all day with their shorts around their ankles?

His wolf didn't like that, and honestly, neither did he.

"I told her I'd wait for her by the door. I think she's puking." Maddi winced, shivering like the thought was enough to make her sick as well. "I made a mistake and ordered pizza for lunch."

"She can't smell pizza, let alone eat it. That goes for melted cheese at all, really. She needs crackers. I know where they are." Jasper took a few steps toward the nearest vending machine before he realized what he'd done. He paused, spinning back around to face Maddi. Her eyes were narrowed, her lips between her teeth. "It's what I heard from Blake, and through the thin bathroom walls at Jace's houses."

"You sperm-filled little bastard." She let out a deep sigh, her shoulders hunching and her head hanging down. "Of course you knocked up the Sunday school teacher."

Jasper nodded, wincing. "We were going to tell you at dinner tonight."

"You told her?" Callie spoke softly behind him. Her voice timid, like she was nervous.

He reached for her hand, guiding her to stand beside him. He squeezed, reassuring her he was here and everything was going to be fine. "I sort of started to lecture her about your melted cheese aversion, and she guessed. She called me a sperm-filled bastard."

"You are." Callie cut her gaze to him briefly before focusing on Maddi. "I'm sorry we lied. It's my fault. Jasper wanted to give me time to figure things out."

"It's not your fault." Jasper shook her hand, which he was still clutching for some reason. "We weren't ready for everyone to know. Now we are, so we're here, telling you." He swung her around to face him. "You don't need to apologize to anyone for anything. Do you understand?" His pack weren't her parents. They wouldn't demand obedience and groveling. He waited for her to nod, then he glanced behind her to Maddi. "We still invited for dinner?"

"Of course." Maddi held her arms out, her bottom lip in a pout. "Get over here, you crazy kids." Jasper pulled Callie with him and let Maddi wrap them into a big, comforting hug. "We're here for whatever you need, okay?"

Jasper smiled, hugging her back.

She'd proved his expectations were right on point. They were going to be supportive. Sure, they might be snarky and slightly worried, but supportive nonetheless.

The three of them walked across campus, Jasper pointing out buildings and sharing funny stories with Callahan about his misspent youth. He told her about the time freshman year he convinced Riley to fill the fountain with dish soap, and how Linc caught them. He'd laughed, taken a video, and then turned them over to Dom for punishment. It was nice to have memories here, anecdotes he could share with her that had nothing to do with the number of, uh, notches in his proverbial bedpost.

"Hey, fuck nut, glad you're here. I made meat loaf." Linc handed him a beer as soon as he stepped into their house. "I've never made meatloaf before, but I think I nailed it." The smell floating through the house and wrinkling Maddi's nose told them that Linc, in fact, had *not* nailed it. "We were out of tomato paste, so I doubled the ketchup. Took a whole bottle, but it looks good to me."

Jasper scooped Allison up off the floor, beating Maddi to snag the first snuggles. He breathed in the sweet scent of her baby shampoo and tickled her tummy so he could hear her tinkling laughter. He loved this kid, and he was good with her. He knew he could handle a baby of his own, and he was beyond appreciative that Maddi and Linc had let him be so hands-on with his cosmic little sister.

He handed her off to her mother with a smirk when she started tapping her foot in annoyance. "Linc?" Jasper headed back into the kitchen, following Linc and the stench of dinner.

"Grab some plates, will ya?" Linc was setting glass dishes crusted with burnt offerings in the center of the dining room table. In addition to the meatloaf, he appeared to have tried his hand at mashed potatoes and maybe, uh, maybe those were green beans? They were floating in some buttery milky substance.

Jasper took four plates out of the cabinet, setting the table while Maddi and Callahan drifted in. He could tell that Callie was trying to breathe through her mouth. He chuckled as he crossed the room and opened a couple windows to help air out the smell. He sat next to her, leaning over to whisper in her ear, "Don't eat anything. We'll go into town on the way home and pick up dinner."

She nodded, reaching for her water and taking a big gulp.

Maddi got Allison set up in her highchair, pulling a box of Cheerios from the pantry and sprinkling some on her tray. Linc frowned. "I made dinner, why are you giving her cereal?"

"I don't want to clean up toddler puke."

Linc gasped, like he was outraged. "Rude."

"There are *lots* of things you are extremely good at, my love. But I don't think meatloaf is one of them." Maddi patted the back of his hand and tossed some of Allison's cereal into her mouth. "Jasper has something to tell you, then I'm sure the two of them are going to get out of here. I'm honestly surprised the burnt ketchup smell hasn't made Callahan gag."

"I'm breathing through my mouth." Callie sent Linc a weak smile. "Meatloaf isn't easy to make. Maybe start with, um, spaghetti? Or like, well, anything that isn't a solid block of meat?"

Linc sent her a droll look, then pursed his lips. "You're getting as snarky as the rest of these assholes, and I like it."

Jasper chuckled, agreeing with Linc. Callahan was really coming into her own. He loved that she was comfortable enough to speak up and give Linc a hard time.

"What do you need to tell me? Did you get arrested? Flunk your first semest—"

"I'm going to be a dad." He cut off Linc, watching with amusement as his jaw dropped dramatically. "I'm the one who got Callie pregnant. So. Yeah. We're having a baby."

"You sperm-filled bastard." Linc sighed, his shoulders sinking like Maddi's had as his attention turned to Callahan. He sent her a small smile. "You fell for his shit?"

Callie laughed lightly, shaking her head. "He worked real hard for it, I assure you."

"You suddenly got jokes?" Jasper squeezed her thigh playfully. Innocent and shy Callahan had drawn him in. Quietly strong Callahan had impressed him beyond measure. A sarcastic Callahan at Maddi's dining room table? Well, that was enough to end him.

Her eyebrows raised, her lips twitching into a smirk he didn't know she was capable of. "Show me the lie? You basically had to beg me to hang out with you, and you sat through hours of tutoring for it. Then you begged me some more to go out with you, and you had to pose it as a group hang to get me to agree."

Jasper scoffed. "Well, I wasn't the one begging in the end, now was I?" He sent her a pointed look, the memory of her soft pleas filling his head. He shifted in his seat, trying to readjust his dick without everyone noticing. His wolf liked his current train of thought, panting for more for the first time since he'd slept with her and made that baby inside her.

"But wait, Callahan, the other night you said you didn't know if you were going to keep the baby."

She nodded. "We decided to co-parent. To raise him, or her." She glanced at him, shrugging before giving her attention back to Linc. "We took our time making our decision, that's why we didn't want to tell anyone right away."

"You're having a baby?" Linc blinked rapidly, like he was still slightly in shock.

Jasper rested his arm along the back of Callahan's chair. "We're having a baby."

"We need to tell the paaaaa...ople, the other people. In this family."

He rolled his eyes at Linc's slip and lame-ass save. He hated the reminder that Callahan was still in the dark. She had no clue she could be pregnant with a little shifter. No idea her life was now tied to a group of supernatural beings.

"Just what Jace will want, hosting another family dinner." Jasper pulled out his cell, texting his twin.

J: *We told Linc and Maddi about the baby. We need to have everyone else over, so we don't have to do an announcement tour all over Haxton.*

"Well, he shouldn't have built a massive mountain estate with a dining room that seats twenty. He created his own worst nightmare." Linc was pushing food around on his plate, pretending he was eating and not fooling anyone.

Jasper's phone vibrated on the table with a response.

Jace: I hate you. But I'll roast a chicken tomorrow night.

"You two get out of here. Callahan looks like she's going to fall asleep sitting up." Maddi stood, plucking Allison from her seat. "I'm going to put this one in the bath while Linc goes to pick up Chinese."

"But I made dinner." Linc pouted.

"You attempted dinner, and I love you for it." Maddi dipped their daughter down so both Jasper and Linc could kiss her cheeks. "You go get food and then we can eat naked. Deal?"

Linc clapped his hands together, getting to his feet. "Fucking deal."

Chapter Twenty-Seven

Callahan

Telling Linc and Maddi Jasper was the father of her baby was way less stressful than she'd anticipated. Jasper's family was so different than hers. They were messy, and it was somewhat chaotic. They loved though. They loved hard. And they supported him—them. Linc and Maddi didn't try to make them feel bad, and they didn't demand anything of them. The thought of telling her parents she was pregnant haunted her. It hung over her head like a black rain cloud. She dreaded it with a gnawing pit in her stomach. Haxton, St. Leasing, had become her sanctuary. The idea of leaving made her want to weep.

She'd come upstairs when they'd gotten home, exhausted and ready to sleep. She'd showered, taking her time, letting the warm water relax her tense muscles. It'd been a day. They'd seen so many kids. The male-to-female ratio was staggering, but they were seeing students from both St. Leasing and the public schools in town. St. Leasing was all boys. Although boys didn't really seem accurate. The teens they'd seen from the private school seemed older than the public school teenagers, more muscular and confident. They had a different presence about them she couldn't put her finger on. She'd assumed the St. Leasing kids moved back to their homes for the summer, but apparently that wasn't always the case. A few of them chose to stay on campus, for various reasons.

She'd blushed when the first one had dropped his shorts. Before assisting Maddi at the clinic, she'd seen two penises in her entire life. Now? She'd seen dozens upon dozens. At least she was desensitized by this point. The naked male form would no longer cause her any shyness.

When she stepped out of the bathroom, steam escaped from the open doorway. Jasper was lying on her bed and was playing some game on his phone, the music lowered to a quiet hum. She was glad he was here.

She shouldn't be.

She'd promised herself she wouldn't come to rely on him. She knew it would only make things harder in the end. They couldn't hide in Haxton forever. Soon they'd go back to Greenly. Soon she'd live on her own, with their child to take care of. No one would be holding her through the night, drying her tears.

Soon, that would be her job as a mother.

"You don't need to sleep in here." She pulled her towel tighter, going into the closet to change into her pajamas. He'd seen her naked, but this wasn't that.

"I know I don't need to. I want to."

She climbed on the bed and folded her hands in her lap, her legs tucked underneath her. "Eventually, we won't be living together, you know? And I don't want to get used to having someone with me all the time. Because I won't. After the baby comes and we figure out a schedule and—"

"Callie, slow down." He moved beside her, taking her face in his hands. "One step, one day at a time. Right now, we're sleeping across the hall from each other. I like to know you two are safe and sound. We can cross all the other scary bridges when we get to them, okay?"

She nodded, lying down and getting comfortable. "In that case, can you rub my back again?" Her request was soft and timid. She knew she shouldn't ask that of him. She'd lectured him about her relying on him, and she was instantly doing it again.

"Chest down, ass out." He clapped his hands together, chuckling at his own joke as he began to rub her lower back and her hips. "Your bones are softening or some shit, that's why everything aches right now."

"Ass out." She hummed disapprovingly under her breath. "Nice."

"I made your first doctor's appointment today. I added it to Maddi's calendar so she knows that I'll be coming to get you Wednesday."

She hummed again, this time blissed out and incapable of words.

"Are you okay with telling the rest of my family? I know Linc sort of made it sound like we didn't have another choice, but we sure as fuck do."

Maddi and Linc had been kind and supportive, even a little excited. She didn't realize how nervous she'd been about people finding out until they'd been so great about it. In theory, she knew Jace, Riley, Axie and Blake all knew, but none of them attempted to talk about it with her. "Do you think everyone will be as cool as Linc and Maddi?"

"Give or take." They turned to face each other, the light from the bathroom shining between them. "No one is going to be an asshole about it. But they'll all have questions and shit."

"Like where we're going to live, how we're going to afford childcare, how we'll finish school, how we'll split custody, how—"

"Yeah, Callie. Questions like that." Jasper had reached over and gently placed his palm on her mouth to cut off her rant. "You're like barely pregnant. We don't need to have all the answers tomorrow, remember?"

She nipped at his hand, not sure why she felt playful when her life choices were literally hanging over her head like gleaming knives. "I don't want to quit school, but I know I'll need to postpone it for a bit." She sighed, already exhausted at the thought of trying to raise a baby and make the Dean's List. She was going to live off coffee, a wing, and prayer.

"I have lots of money." He chuckled when she snorted at his admission. "I'm not trying to sound like a douche, it's a fact, okay?" She rolled her eyes and he laughed louder. "What I meant to say was, I don't want you to have to postpone your degree. I'll happily pay for childcare while we finish college." He tickled her ribs. "That sound better?"

"A little." She rested her cheek on the back of her hands. "But I want things to be equal."

"They will be," he assured her, his fingers dancing up her bare arm to ruffle her hair. "I don't got the boobs or the vag. Let me pay for childcare as an apology for what my kid is going to do to your banging body."

She giggled, despite herself, her cheeks heating at his teasing. "Sometimes, I think we're going to be okay." And sometimes she was utterly terrified. It'd been a crazy few weeks full of emotional upheavals and changes. She was surrounded by strangers who were becoming friends. Every night, she slept next to a gorgeous boy who was quickly becoming a man.

"Sometimes, I do too, Callie baby." He held out his arm, and for some reason she didn't hesitate. She let him pull her close.

She breathed in his scent and closed her eyes, falling asleep with a soft smile on her face.

Chapter Twenty-Eight

Jasper

Jace complained about having the whole pack over, about having his fortress invaded yet again. It happened every time. He'd act put out, but then he'd spend seven hours preparing a meal that belonged in a fancy restaurant. Case in point, he had in fact roasted a whole-ass chicken the size of a turkey. Then he'd gone above and beyond, pairing it with a salad course, homemade sourdough rolls, and some sort of herbed wild rice.

"Don't pussy out." Linc was sitting to his left, Callie to his right. Linc had been whispering to him since the pack sat down to dinner. He was like a gossipy old lady, anticipating the moment Jasper stood up and told his family he was the father of Callie's baby. "You better not be a little bitch about it."

Jasper rolled his eyes, using his fork to stab the back of Linc's hand. He didn't draw blood, but Linc yelped anyway. "Stop fucking rushing me."

Callie rested her warm hand on his thigh, and his stupid dick decided it liked that.

"You okay?" His wolf seemed to enjoy her touch as well. His wolf was fully awake now, instead of napping here and there. He was a constant presence under Jasper's skin once again. He hadn't realized how much he'd missed the spirit of his wolf. The constant supernatural hum that ran through his veins.

It'd happened so slowly once he'd moved away from his pack that he'd barely noticed until it was too late. He understood now what Riley had gone through. Pen had explained it to them in detail about the pack bolstering their inner wolf and how being isolated suppressed it. Either way, his shifter was back and he liked Callahan. Not in a way that screamed fuck her against a wall and claim her; it was more of a warm light in his heart.

Love. His wolf loved her, he supposed. She was carrying his baby. What wasn't to love?

"Linc's being an impatient prick." He leaned closer to her, not caring that people could clearly see their closeness. "I'm nervous. I know it's silly, but I am." He knew this was his life now and this was what he'd chosen. What they'd chosen. Still. He was anxious.

"Take your time." She patted his thigh, then leaned forward and sent a piercing glare to Linc.

Jasper chuckled, loving she was no longer shy with his invasive species of a family. Sink or swim, and Axie, who was an expert at swimming with sharks, was training Callie for the gold. If she was brave enough to take on a house full of strangers, then he could get through one tiny, life-altering announcement.

He put his fork down, letting it clatter obnoxiously on his plate, causing all eyes to move to him. "I have something to say, to tell you." He cleared his throat. "I, um, I'm the dad. Of the baby. Of Callahan's baby. It's mine. The baby is mine. Ours. The baby is ours and we're going to raise it together. But not like, *together*, you know?"

Everyone was silent, staring at him and at her. This group at a loss for words? That had to be a first. Callie's hand was still on his thigh, so he threaded his fingers through hers, squeezing.

Their eyes met, she smiled. He winked.

And the table erupted into chaos.

Dom and Baze pulled out their wallets and passed cash to Keller. Jace put his head in his hands, most likely hoping everyone would leave and take their noise with them. Riley had his arm around

Blake, both of them trying to explain things to Corey, who'd come back into the room from changing Hadley in the middle of Jasper's awkward speech. Molly was wrangling the twins, shooting rapid-fire questions at Maddi.

Jasper sighed, leaning back in his chair, oddly at ease now that it was out there. It was as if a huge weight had come off his shoulders. They'd made a choice together, and his pack was informed. He needed to call his mom and stepdad, but he knew she'd be more excited than concerned. He rested his arm around the back of Callie's chair, putting his lips near her ear. "You want to get out of here?"

She was blinking rapidly, looking from person to person, as if she was trying to gauge everyone's mood through the mele. "Are we allowed to bail in the middle of this mess? I don't think your brother would like that."

She had a point. Jace would kick his ass for imploding dinner and then throwing up the deuces. See? She was really coming into her own and learning how to survive in the pack...without actually knowing about the pack.

Geez. He'd almost forgotten for a damn second that he was supernatural and the mother of his child had no freaking clue. Full-on exhaustion overtook him, and he became increasingly annoyed with everyone talking over each other, but not actually talking to *him*. Was he hormonal too? His wolf was starting to claw to the surface, wanting him to get the girl carrying his seed away from all the chaos. *Seed?* That was fucking weird. Was his wolf aging at a rapid rate?

"Hey." He stood, using his outside voice to get the pack's attention. "One at a time, or I throw Callie over my shoulder and no one gets any answers. Understood?"

"Huh. Speaking like a dad already." Riley grinned from across the table.

"Are you two, uh, *dating*?" Dom put a hell of a lot of emphasis on the word "dating," and Jasper caught his drift. Dom was asking if Callie was his mate, his forever.

"No." Jasper rested his hands on Callie's shoulders, wanting to make sure his words didn't come out harsh or cruel. "We hooked up one night. We were super careful and responsible." He shrugged. "It happened anyway. We've decided to raise the baby together, as *friends*."

Corey was standing on the other side of the room, trying to corral her and Dom's toddler. "What about school?"

"They'll both finish school," Jace answered before he or Callie got the chance. "I've already looked into childcare in Greenly and put the baby on some waiting lists."

Callie dipped her head back, a frown on her pretty lips when their eyes met. Jasper gave her a slight shake of his head, silently begging her to let Jace's control issues go for the time being. That was a whole other conversation that would need to happen, but not here, and not now.

He wouldn't be surprised if Jace had already purchased Callahan her own house, you know, as another "investment" property.

"So you aren't Blake's friend?" Pen glanced between Callie and Blake. "That wasn't true?"

"Of course we're friends." Blake smiled at Callie, which made Jasper incredibly happy. He loved watching the people he cared for continue to grow closer. "We're friends, but I'm not the one who came up with the plan to stay in Haxton for the summer."

"That was my idea." Jasper supposed he could start answering some more of these questions, although everyone else was doing a great job. "Callie couldn't go home."

"Why?" Molly's lip was out in a pout, like she was seriously concerned for the pregnant teenager she'd only met a few weeks ago. "Did something happen with your parents?"

"My parents, well, they wouldn't be supportive. They *won't* be supportive of us choosing to raise the baby together. They're super religious. My father is a pastor, and this..." She placed both her hands on her stomach, on the baby, their baby. "This is a sin. They'd want us to get married, or they'd want to hide my pregnancy, and then they'd push adoption." She swallowed thickly, and his heart broke a little. He hadn't met her parents yet, but he hated them. "Jasper suggested we come here for a couple months, give ourselves some time to figure it all out."

"And you have? You've decided to parent together?" Baze had been quiet, allowing everyone else to react. Jasper knew their alpha, knew how he worked. He waited to hear and assimilate the actions and chatter of the pack. He needed to assess the situation and draw his own conclusions. He needed to gauge how this would affect their dynamic, how this would alter their future. "Boy *or* girl."

"Yes." Baze was asking if Jasper's desire to keep the baby was because he thought it was a boy, a shifter-to-be. He didn't care though, girl or boy, shifter or not. He was going to be a dad. "Again. We're keeping the baby."

"Okay. Well then, congratulations?" Baze raised an eyebrow.

Jasper couldn't help but smile. Baze was the first one to say that, to acknowledge that maybe this was something worth celebrating. It wasn't going to be easy, and it wasn't ideal. But Jasper was having a baby. He was going to be a dad. And fuck, that was actually incredibly cool. "Thank you."

The rest of the pack followed Baze's lead. They passed out hugs and kind words, and they surrounded Callie in warmth and support.

They offered to help with doctor's appointments and baby showers.

They were everything he told Callie they would be.

Chapter Twenty-Nine

Jasper

Wednesday. Hump day. Although he wasn't going to be humping anytime soon, he supposed. With his wolf being back in full force, he expected it to want him to go out on the prowl. Not in a creepy rapey sort of way. His wolf liked the hunt, the game. He supposed that was why he'd been down to work so hard to get Callahan to notice him.

Interestingly, the shifter living under his skin seemed pretty content at the moment. The only time he pushed his authority was when Callie was around. He wanted her safe because he wanted the baby safe and happy. It was instinctual.

Jasper didn't mind. For the most part, he felt the same way.

Callie was at the clinic with Maddi. She had her first doctor's appointment later that afternoon. He was going to pick her up and take her there himself. He found he was actually excited to see the baby for the first time. He knew it was healthy and growing. He could feel its presence, hear its fluttering heartbeat.

"Get in here." Baze reached his hand out of Jace's office, dragging Jasper inside by the sleeve of his shirt. He'd been on his way to the basement for a workout. Guess that would have to wait.

Baze, Jace, and Riley were in the office. Jace was behind his desk, and Riley was leaning under the window with his hands in his pockets, while their pack alpha shoved Jasper into a chair with half strength.

"Is this an intervention of some sort?"

Baze ignored Jasper's attempt at a joke. "Last night was one thing, but today is another. I have questions, and you're going to sit your little ass down and answer every single one of them." His alpha tone wiped all rapidly forming thoughts of resistance out of Jasper's brain. There was no fighting the pack dynamic, especially when the alpha and the beta were teaming up against him.

"Let's hear it then." Jasper gestured for Baze to continue. He had shit to do, and he hadn't planned on this ass chewing when he'd mapped out his day.

"You leave here for one damn semester and you get someone pregnant? Are you fucking kidding me? How did this happen?" Jasper was irritated at Baze's mood, at his demanding questions. He was also pissed as hell Baze had basically lured him into a false sense of security last night. Sneaky prick with his congratulations and kind smiles. "Answer me."

He didn't bother making any jokes about the how of creating a baby. He didn't think Baze would appreciate that, and he wasn't ready for a pop to the back of his head at the moment.

"We met in class, and when I hit on her, she turned me down. A few times." He didn't need to note he didn't typically get turned down, ever. They all knew that about him. "So, I changed my game plan and I asked her to tutor me instead. She's brilliant and she didn't want to give me the time of day. I was into the chase. You know how it goes. I, uh, wore her down. We went out, we hooked up. It was one night and I was careful. I wrapped it up, several times." He threw up his hands, letting them fall to smack down into his lap. "I didn't intentionally knock her up, obviously."

"You sure you're the father?" Baze. Again. Asshole. He didn't like Baze's accusation; neither did his wolf. He had to work hard to keep a growl from forming in his chest.

He glanced past his alpha, to Jace, his twin, and the pack beta. Jace didn't offer a way out, he simply crossed his arms over his chest. Jasper swallowed the snarl still threatening to break free.

"Riley ran into Callahan on campus a couple of weeks after we hooked up, he sensed the baby. He came home and told me, so I called her and invited her over to the house for dinner. She didn't know she was pregnant 'til that night. I took her to get a test, and I sat with her after she took it. I was there for her initial reaction. I asked if it was mine, she said yes. I believe her, one hundred percent, no doubt."

"I've spent the better part of a month with her. Callahan isn't lying. She doesn't have it in her." Jace finally spoke up, and it was to defend Callie.

Jasper and his wolf liked that, a lot.

Riley shoved off from his spot against the wall. With all the alpha and beta energy clogging the room, Jasper had almost forgotten he was here. "Jasper stepped up the moment I told him about the baby. He stepped up." Jasper ignored the emotion making his throat swell. "He's done everything right. Everything he can to help Callahan."

"She didn't want me, not at first. I worked my ass off to get her into my bed, seems only fair I work my ass off to be a good guy for her. And the baby."

Baze studied him, his hands on his hips. "You sure she isn't your mate?"

The same question he'd been asked by his best friends, by his brother. He wished his answer had changed. "I wish she was, man. I really do. She's smart, beautiful, and strong as hell. But no. She's not for me. I'd know by now. I'd have to."

"Okay. Well, raising this kid with her means you have to bring her into the fold, and soon."

He knew Baze was right, but Jasper wasn't ready. It was a huge secret to reveal. Her life had already changed so much in the last few weeks. Finding out shifters were real, that the guy she'd had sex with turned into an actual wolf? That was a lot. "I'll tell her soon. Definitely before the baby is born."

That gave him a nice seven-month win—

"Don't you think that's information she deserves *now*? What if she can't handle it and she changes her mind about you or about raising the baby herself?" Riley held out his hands palms up when a low growl erupted from Jasper's throat. "I'm not trying to be a dick, man. I'm spouting facts, and you know it."

"You said it yourself, she isn't yours," Jace said. "If she wasn't made for this life, made to love a shifter, then she might react really fucking badly." Jace got up from his space behind his desk, coming around to join Riley and Baze.

Now all three of them were standing in front of Jasper. He hated what they were saying, and he hated that they were right.

He cracked his neck side to side, taking a few deep breaths while he waited for his wolf to settle and his thoughts to arrange themselves correctly. In the back of his mind, he'd known what they were saying was a possibility. It was hard to think about, to face, so he'd pushed it away. Ignored it.

"If she doesn't want me or the pack in her life, then I'll fight for joint custody." Jasper stood, his body rigid, repelling the notion of battling Callahan in court. "I made my choice about the baby, and I have rights too." His wolf would never let him back out of his decision about the baby, and neither would his human heart.

"Whoa." Riley sat back, perching his ass on the edge of Jace's desk. "You really do want this kid?"

"Of course I want my kid." Jasper shook his head in disbelief. "I know I'm the fuck-up, the good time. But I'm not dicking around with this." He put his hand to his chest. "Did you think I was lying? Did you think I told her I'd help raise the baby as some kind of game? To what end?"

"No, man. That's not what I meant." Riley reached out, putting his palm on Jasper's shoulder. "I just, I guess hearing you be so protective, so willing to go to bat for your paternal rights. Damn. You're really going to be a dad. Like you're a dad already."

Jace moved back behind his desk, sitting down and clicking around the keyboard. "I'm sending you a file I compiled once you told me you wanted to keep the kid." He hit one more button with flourish. "It's a list of daycares he's on the list for, as well as profiles of some nannies in case you want to go that route. They're old and married. I figured it would complicate things if you started fucking the chicks you pay to help with your son."

"Uh, thanks, but you've gotta chill with that shit. Callie isn't used to having you run her life." His phone vibrated in his pocket, alerting him of the information his twin sent. "And why do you assume the baby is a boy? You guys know something I don't?" He glanced from face to face, stopping on Riley. "Why are you smiling like that?"

"Congrats, bro, it's a boy." Riley held his hand out for a high five, then pulled Jasper in for a hug.

"Are you serious? How can you tell and I can't? It's my kid. I figured my supernatural shit would be in hyperdrive or something." Jasper could hear the heartbeat and sense the baby growing. Out of everyone in the pack, Riley had always been the best at getting a feel for the details when it came to the early stages of pregnancy.

Riley let him go, a goofy grin on his face. "I don't know how, but I can tell he's a little shifter in the making. Can't explain it, never can. It just is."

Jasper had great examples of fathers around him all the time. He'd been lucky enough to spend his childhood with his mother and stepdad, Charlie.

When he got to St. Leasing, he'd had all his coaches as role models.

"Well, shit. I'm going to have a son."

Chapter Thirty

Callahan

Their first doctor's appointment went well. The baby was growing and was healthy. They heard the heartbeat, neither one of them cried like those overjoyed couples in the movies. True to his word, though, Jasper had been next to her every step of the way. He even insisted on staying in the room for the pelvic exam. They compromised and he stood up by her head. Sure, he'd seen her naked, but spread out with her feet in stirrups wasn't the same thing.

He dropped her back off at the clinic afterward. Maddi held extended hours for working parents a few times a month and Callahan easily lost herself in the ebb and flow of their patient-filled evening. They were supposed to do only physicals, to clear players as eligible to play sports. It never failed though, either the kids or their parents would ask for medical advice, or for them to treat small scrapes and injuries. She loved that each appointment had the potential to bring something new.

Callahan hadn't given much thought yet to what she wanted to major in, or which career path to take, but nursing or something in the medical field was looking like an exciting possibility.

"You're home. Did you eat?" Blake and Axie were on the couch, a giant bowl of popcorn between them and an ominous-sounding movie on the TV. "The guys went out for a run."

Callahan hung her bag on the hook in the hallway before joining them in the living room. "It's not odd to you two that they always go out to run after the sun goes down?"

"It's cooler outside that way." Blake spoke around a mouthful of popcorn and butter.

"It's Colorado." Callahan glanced at the backyard, the high that day hadn't even reached eighty degrees. "And they only run at night." It was something she'd thought was strange at first, and now it was downright bothering her. Jasper always brushed off her concern and questions, and it seemed Axie and Blake were doing the same thing.

"Boys are weird." Axie waved away her observations, shoving popcorn into her mouth as well. "We're watching scary movies." She patted the cushion next to her. "Does powdered cheese bother you, or just melted? Blake dumped a whole bottle of the powered crap over the top of this popcorn like a savage."

"I can go make you your own bowl." Blake hopped up, dusting her hands on her yoga pants and leaving an orange smear.

"No, you don't need to do that." Callahan sat down beside Axie. "I ate a really late lunch with Maddi. I'm not really hungry."

"Yeah, but if Jasper finds out we didn't try to feed his baby mama, he'll get all pissy." Blake made her way into the kitchen and then came back tossing a banana her way. She held up a jar of peanut butter with a wink. "I hear this is your fav."

She settled in beside her new friends and peeled the banana, dunking it into the peanut butter and trying to figure out what their ridiculous movie was even about. There was a clown, but like cotton candy cocoons and a spaceship? As she was about to start asking questions, the patio doors opened and three sweaty men walked into the room.

Jasper's chest was heaving, like he'd only stopped running once he reached the yard. His skin was glistening and she could smell his yummy scent from all the way across the room. "You're home. Did you eat?"

She held up her banana as Blake snickered beside her. "Told you."

"Told her what?" He came farther into the room, wiping his face with a towel. Jace picked up Axie and placed her in his lap while Riley came out of the kitchen draining a large bottle of water. He glanced down at the tub of popcorn and made a face of disapproval, which Blake promptly ignored.

"I told her we had to feed her or you'd get pissy." Blake palmed more popcorn into her mouth, smiling at Riley while she chewed messily.

Callahan could feel Jasper's gaze on her, smell his scent. She was afraid to look at him, half dressed and gorgeous. She was having a harder and harder time trying to control her hormones when it came to him.

She knew how good he could make her body feel. She knew how amazing it would be. She also knew with sex came consequences, and some of those consequences were too high a price to pay. He already slept in her bed every night, rubbing her hips until she fell asleep. She refused to blur those lines even more by giving in to her silly whims.

"Do you want something else other than that or are you ready for bed?" He glanced down at his watch, the movement making her gaze jump to his dumb biceps. "I want to shower, but then I can come rub your back."

"I'm fine." She got to her feet, feeling out of sorts in a way she wasn't used to. "I'm full, and yeah, I am really beat. It was a long day. I'm going to go ahead and get to bed." He took a step, like he was going to follow her, so she held a hand out to stop him. "No. You take your time or shower, or uh, I don't need...I'm fine. My back is great. Thanks."

She left the room while not making eye contact with a single one of them on her way up the stairs. She was acting insane. She sounded insane. She knew that. She couldn't stay downstairs and play the fifth wheel, or worse have Jasper come sit next to her and start rubbing her hips or trying to make her smile.

Even him caring whether she'd eaten, it was too much. She couldn't start to fall in lust *or* love with the father of her child. They agreed to co-parents and shit, she thought as she rolled her eyes.

That was the agreed-upon plan and she refused to be the one to mess it all up. Life was already too complicated.

"Hey, what was that? Are you okay?" Jasper was in her doorway, having followed her whether she wanted him to or not.

Childishly, she put her hand over her eyes, holding out a hand again to try to stop him from getting any closer to her or her hormones. "I'm fine."

"Callie, you're curled up on the bed with one had over your eyes and a peanut butter banana in the other." She felt the bed dip, damn him. "You don't seem fine." He pulled her palm from her face, a playful smirk on his face. "What's going on?"

She looked at him, really looked at him.

It was an indulgence, and one she should've continued to avoid if she knew what was good for her.

His shirt was still off, his hair a disheveled mess. He was tan and put together in the most perfect way. Gorgeous. No doubt about it. He knew what to do with everything he had going on too.

More and more often, she was recalling their night together. She'd feel her temperature start to rise. She now knew what desire felt like and it was hard to ignore. Harder still with him in front of her being sweet and offering to rub her down as she fell asleep.

She was hormonal and constantly unsure of her next move, which was proving to be an intoxicating mix.

Chapter Thirty-One

Jasper

Jasper had come back from his run happy to see Callie was home safe and sound, and eating. His wolf had a thing about making sure she fed the baby. His wolf had increasing demands when it came to their offspring. Then she seemed to lose her cool a bit and she all but sprinted up the stairs to her room. He'd followed her to make sure she was okay, and also to make sure she didn't end up tripping on the stairs in her rush.

He tried not to laugh as she put both palms over her eyes once again. "Can you not, um, can you put a shirt on?" Her heart was pounding, he could hear it. She was sweating too, but she did that sometimes. He figured it was the pregnancy. The hormones and the changes in her body. This though, what was going on tonight, this was different. She was flushed and her pulse was racing, her breathing shallow. Now she was asking him to put a shirt on? If he didn't know any better....

"Are you turned on right now?" He couldn't help the smirk on his face. She was stunning, and he'd wanted her again two beats after she'd climbed out of his bed all those weeks ago.

He'd jacked off over and over to the memory of them and their one night together. He hadn't hit on her, and he hadn't tried anything.

She was pregnant. They were going through so much while trying to figure out their future. For once in his life, he'd wanted to do right by someone. He wanted to be who she needed.

But if what she needed was a good fucking, he'd sure as hell deliver. "Callie?"

"I, uh, no. It's not that. I don't, um, that doesn't happen."

"Horny *and* shuddering?" He licked his lips. "Damn, baby."

She swallowed thickly, letting her hands fall to her lap as she kept her pretty deep green eyes closed. "I am not *horny*," she whispered that last word like she embarrassed to say it, let alone feel it. "These pregnancy hormones are wrecking my mind and my body, and sometimes when I look at you, I appreciate that, well, you're attractive. Okay? You're gorgeous and I don't have control over my body at the moment, and it would help if you wouldn't come in here half naked and smirking."

"Callie." He found her rambling both flattering and adorable. He scooted closer, placing his palms on her cheeks. "We're a team, yeah?" She nodded. "When someone brings melted cheese into the house, I take care of it, right?" She nodded again. "The way you're feeling right now, the things you want, I can take care of that too."

"We shouldn't cross that line again." She shook her hair, the red locks moving across her chest. "Blurring the boundaries of what this is, of what we are, it's not smart."

It wasn't smart; in fact, he knew it was utterly stupid. However, he'd be damned if he left her alone feeling empty and unfulfilled. It's not like he'd let her go into town and find some random shithead to hook up with. That was his kid in there.

"You've got months of pregnancy hormones ahead of you. Let me help."

She winced. "You're making it sound like a chore."

Jasper threw his head back, laughing loudly. "A chore? Oh hell no." He also found it entertaining she couldn't say sex, or fucking. *It.* That was how she was referring to their situation. "It would be my pleasure. I swear to you." He moved his hand to the column of her slender throat. "I don't just want you. I *crave* you. I touch myself all the damn time to the memory of your body moving underneath mine. The way I filled you up, the sweet little sounds you made. Fuck, Callie. Let me do this for you, for both of us."

"Okay."

"Yeah?"

She nodded, her chest heaving.

That was all the permission he needed.

He used his grip to pull her closer, fusing his lips to hers. He hummed in satisfaction, rising on his knees to change the angle of their kiss.

She opened for him, lying back down on the pillows, her thighs parting to welcome him. He pressed his body against hers, groaning the second his cock touched her core, even with all the clothes between them.

She was writhing underneath him, pulling at the drawstring of his shorts. All her hesitation had vanished; she was nothing but a whimpering mess and he fucking loved it.

He pushed back, using one hand to pull her panties down her legs, only bothering to get one leg free. He wanted inside her, he wanted to take his time, to savor her.

But it was impossible, his need was too consuming. He trailed his palm up to her thigh, pushing it to the mattress as she freed his length. They were moving fast, both overcome with a want they didn't know they'd been keeping at bay.

He slid inside her heat, groaning at how perfect she felt. "Fuck, Callie." He buried his face in her neck, nipping and lapping at her skin. He'd never been with anyone like this, with no barrier.

He'd waited his whole life, thinking he'd save this part of himself for his mate. His forever. "I've never." He didn't need to finish his thought. He knew she understood.

Her nails were digging into his biceps, her hips rising to meet his. She was panting, her heart pounding at a rhythm that matched his own. He stared down at her, watching as her eyes closed and her lips parted. "More."

He rose, one hand going to her thigh and one tightening on her throat. He surged inside her, pushing as far as he could go. He felt like he couldn't possibly get deep enough. He wanted to fuck her soul.

Something fractured in his chest. A shiver traveled down his spine as his heart splintered wide open. The animal inside him came to life, fighting him for control. *Mine.*

He tensed, trying like hell to push his shifter back down into the depths where he'd been so content moments before.

It was no use.

His wolf took over, thrusting into her over and over, hard and intense. Jasper started to panic, but it was too late; he wasn't in control anymore. His vision blurred, his spine tingling, his body vibrating, the magic building.

"Baby, look at me." The command in his tone shocked him.

Callie opened her eyes, connecting with his. He was screaming in his mind, at war with himself in a way he'd never experienced. He wanted to save her, to stop this before it was too late.

"Stop me, Callie. Make this stop."

She didn't get it. She gripped him tighter, not allowing him to leave her body, not an inch. "No, don't stop, please don't stop." He was powerless to the animal he shared his body with and the girl he didn't know was his. "More."

He'd never felt pleasure like this. Every drag of his cock inside Callie was utter ecstasy. "Fuck, baby, this..." He wanted to tell her this wasn't right. This wasn't what she wanted or deserved. She didn't know what she was asking of him.

Mine. Ours.

He lost.

He held her gaze, enthralled with the way she shattered around him as he spilled everything he was inside her perfect body.

The air shimmered around them, the universe binding them to each other in an unbreakable bond.

She belonged to him, now and forever.

Chapter Thirty-Two

Jasper

Jasper lay there, holding her in his arms until her breathing had evened out and her body went fully limp. It didn't take long. He'd given her the *really* good dick. Unfortunately, he'd also given her his fucking soul. He left her sleeping peacefully in bed.

Holy shit.

He didn't know the bonding would happen. He screamed at the stupid wolf inside him, strutting around like a happy fucker. *What was that? A little heads-up would've been nice.*

He'd had zero inclination that she was his, that Callie was his forever. When he came with nothing between them, he'd felt it. His entire world shifted, shimmering and blurring around the edges. His heart expanded, and his soul seemed to have left his body for actual moments.

He'd never come so fucking hard in his life. His balls ached.

He slipped out of bed, pulling his cell from his pocket, his hands shaking as he tried to type out a text to his group chat with Riley and Jace.

J: *I need help. Meet me downstairs. Uh, 911 or SOS or whatever gets you fuckers to put your dicks away.*

He pressed a kiss to Callie's temple, pulling the covers tighter around her. Without his body heat, she'd get cold. He kicked off the blankets every night and it always made her spoon deeper into his warmth.

He sighed, tiptoeing out of the room and shutting the door quietly behind him.

He made his way quietly down to the living room, thankful for Jace's pretentious yet always stocked bar cart. He poured himself a glass of whiskey, drinking it in one swallow and then pouring another.

"This better be an actual emergency." Riley scrubbed his hands down his face. "I did, in fact, have my dick out."

"Fuck. Fuck. Shit." Jasper pulled at his hair frantically, finally allowing his freak-out to fully set in now that Riley was present. He could hear Jace making his way into the room. "I fucked up. I fucked up bad."

"For the love of everything holy, spit out what the hell you did." Jace sat down heavy on his couch, rolling his eyes at Jasper's antics. "This is why I hate houseguests by the way."

"I had sex with Callie."

Riley snorted out a quick laugh. "Yeah, no shit."

"No." Jasper stood still, his heart pounding. "Like again, and without a condom this time."

Jace rested his head on his fist. "Well, she's already pregnant, what would a condom help at this point?"

"I didn't, fuck, I didn't think she was mine. I thought I was possessive of the baby, and that it had nothing to do with her. But then she was horny, and I'm always horny, so I figured, why the hell not? What's the worst that could happen?"

He started pacing again. "I grabbed her by the throat and like, held her in place like a fucking pyscho and made her look at me and—"

"You claimed her." Jace sat up, clearly ready to pay attention.

Jasper stopped moving, his back sliding down the wall where he collapsed on the floor, his head in his hands and his empty glass between his fingers. "I claimed her."

"I told you so." Riley had a smirk on his face when Jasper glanced up with a sneer. "I had to say it once, you know I did." He hung his head back down. "Look, this is a good thing. The mother of your child is meant to be yours, your forever. This is right, this is fate. It's everything." Riley moved to the bar cart, pouring himself a drink. "You won't have to worry about her running away or having to fight for custody. Problem solved." He saluted Jasper with his whiskey, a silent toast.

Jasper banged his skull against the wall a few times before nodding slowly. "Except Callie knows nothing about our world. She doesn't know she's now mated, without her permission, to a shifter. She doesn't know she's carrying a mini one inside her. We agreed to co-parent as friends, and now, she's my entire fucking universe."

"Well, maybe we should have Keller come over? He accidentally claimed Molly, right? And they're okay." Riley moved over to the couch, sitting beside a scowling Jace.

"No. No more company," Jace ordered. "This house is closed."

"Yeah, bro, and the last thing I want to do is bring all the coaches into this shitstorm." Jasper knew if he really did want Keller's involvement, his twin would swallow his irritation and get him over here. Middle of the night or not.

"Riley's right. Not about inviting every fucking pack member to this house for no reason, but about Keller and Molly." Jace held his hand out, asking Riley for his half full tumbler. He threw it down his throat before continuing. "Keller freaked when he mated Molly."

"Oh, he freaked big time. I was there." Riley chuckled at the memory. "He and Dom were taking shots and getting wasted at like six o'clock in the morning."

"But he spazzed for no reason. Molly was fine, eventually, because she was made for him." Jace met his gaze from his sad spot on the floor. "The same thing with Corey. She didn't overreact when Dom shifted in front of her because she was made for this life, fated to be mated to a shifter."

"Blake too." Riley shrugged. "She took it all in stride."

"None of them were pregnant at nineteen." Jasper finally got to his feet. "Callie is already going through so fucking much. She's stressed about everything. She's nervous to tell her parents about the baby. And now it's not just *hey I'm a shifter and so is our kid*. It's, *hey I'm a shifter, and so is our kid oh and btdub when we fucked the other night I accidentally claimed you as mine and now you hold my life in your innocent little hands*."

"Holy fuck, I *knew* it." Blake clapped her hands and did a silly happy dance. "I knew she was yours. For freaking shifters, you guys have terrible gut instincts."

"Jesus H. Christ." Jasper sighed. "When the hell did you sneak down here?"

She shrugged, vaulting over the back of the couch and settling against Riley's side. "I got bored, so I came down here to get a snack and see what Axie was doing but this is *sooooo* much better." She rubbed her hands together. "Tell me everything."

"Wait, not yet. Wait for me." Axie came into the room, perching on Jace's lap with yet another giant bowl of popcorn in her hands. She shoved some in her mouth, then passed it to Blake, talking around it. "Okay, I'm ready."

"I hate you both." Jasper collapsed on the loveseat opposite the two couples.

"Liar." Axie rolled her eyes. "You love us. Now tell us the whole story. Don't leave out any of the juicy details."

"You've both been claimed before, you know how it goes." He rested his head back, staring at the ceiling. "I banged her. I figured a condom was unnecessary. My wolf showed pretty quick, I tried to stop him, he told me to fuck the hell off and then right before I busted a nut, I pinned her down and made her look at me. She seemed into it, she screamed real fucking loud, so there's that. But then my whole world blurred and my heart was racing. I knew it was happening, but there was nothing I could do to stop it."

"Where is she now? You left her up there to come have bro time?" Blake glanced behind her, like maybe he'd stashed her somewhere close by. "That's rude."

He picked up his head, stressed, but still himself. He smirked. "I worked her over real fucking good. She passed out pretty quick."

Blake snorted. "It's not your dick that knocked her out. Don't flatter yourself. She's fucking pregnant and working full days with Maddi."

"Oh yeah? My dick knocked your—"

"Nope." Riley threw a handful of popcorn at him. "You promised you wouldn't talk about the cabin 'til January. Keep your damn mouth shut."

Blake sent him a snotty smile. "Besides, it took *two* dicks to knock me out that night." Axie reached over and high-fived her, Jace pulled his mate's hand back, scolding her with a shake of his head.

"For shit's sake, doll, can you not?" Riley tickled her ribs, making her squirm in his lap.

She giggled through her words. "I figured I need to get a couple hits in now, because I can promise you, those jokes about the cabin are going to come to a screeching halt." Her gaze moved across the room, training on him. "Or do you want sweet innocent Callahan to know that you double-teamed your best friend's girlfriend, who you live with?"

"Ooooooo, good point."

Riley ignored Axie. "You're my *mate*. Not my girlfriend." He frowned. "I thought we at least agreed to say fiancée."

Jasper swallowed past a new lump in his throat. "Holy shit, you're right. She has no clue about any of the shit Riley and I used to do. Or the fact my dick has been in your—"

"No." Riley raised his voice, cutting off Jasper from saying another word. "That's enough. It's late as hell, your frantic bitch-ass text literally pulled me out of my girl, and I'm not going to sit down here and listen to your shit."

"Are you going to tell her?" Axie shoveled another handful of popcorn into her mouth, completely ignoring Riley's irritation. "About what a whore you were?"

Blake reached over, grabbing some of the offered midnight snack. "She knows some of his rep. Why do you think she kept turning him down? She was on campus with us for a full semester and she definitely was not the first girl you banged. Just the only one you knocked up. Right?"

Everyone sort of looked at each other, blinking in silence, letting the thought of Jasper getting more than one coed pregnant settle between them. No one seemed to want to touch it, thankfully.

He didn't want to cause any issues between Blake and Callie. He liked the way their relationship was developing. Their closeness made him happy. Callie would need Blake's support, and Axie's as well. The thought of putting a strain on their friendship sucked.

He held out his hand, caching the bowl when Axie slid it across the coffee table. "So what should I tell her first? That I had anal with her one of her only friends, that I turn into a wolf at will, or that she's my mate and I claimed her by accident?" He pushed some popcorn into his mouth as his brain threatened to shut down.

"I'd lead with wolf, then give it a few days to settle." Jace stood, setting his girl on her feet. "Then tell her a little about our culture and the other couples in the pack. After she grasps that, you can let her know she's your forever." He took Axie's hand, dragging her out of the living room and calling over his shoulder, "And then, maybe mention that you used to like it when Riley pulled out his dick." Axie's laughter echoed as they made their way back to their bedroom.

The remaining couple got up, making their way to the stairs. "I agree with Jace." Blake patted him on the back. "Let us know how we can help, okay?"

He appreciated her offer. He wasn't sure how they could help, not at first. Maybe once he'd laid it all out there, placed the truth at Callie's feet, Axie and Blake could provide some moral support.

He paused at Callie's door, turning to tell them thank you. He didn't get the words out though, because Riley punched him right in the fucking face. He stumbled back, catching himself on the wall.

"You deserved that." Riley ruffled his hair. "If you ever utter the word *anal* in my presence again, I'll break your nose."

Jasper nodded, heading back downstairs in search of some ice for his cheek. "Fair enough."

Chapter Thirty-Three

Callahan

Callahan didn't mean to have sex with Jasper. She wasn't sure what had come over her, what had made her feel so flushed, so utterly honest. That wasn't who she was. She didn't talk about sex and hormones and lust. Jasper did though, so unapologetically. It was intoxicating, the ease in which he articulated the things he needed, what he wanted. Still. Having sex with the father of her baby wasn't a smart move. She'd woken up early and embarrassed. She was nervous, unsure of what Jasper's attitude would be in the light of day. They'd been scratching an itch, right?

And scratch it they had. She thought her mind had been blown the first time they were together. That was nothing compared to last night. Jasper seemed to be inside her brain or something. He knew exactly what she needed and how to give it to her.

"Callie? You okay?"

"Sorry. Did you say something?" She smiled at Maddi, handing her a tablet containing the next patient's medical history and release form. "I was just, um, getting these next few kids uploaded."

Maddi took the tablet, a suspicious grin on her face. "You sure you're okay? You seem a little spacey today. A little distracted."

"Oh, uh, I apologize. I didn't mean to cause any problems."

"Whoa, no, sweet girl. That's not what I meant." Maddi reached for her hand, guiding her away from the waiting area and the thinning crowd of teenage boys. "You are a rock star. I don't know how I would be pulling any of this off without you. I was concerned. I wanted to make sure that everything was okay, that's all."

Callahan found herself wanting to confide in Maddi, to tell her what happened last night and how confused about everything she was. She couldn't ever talk to her mom about stuff like that. She put her hand to her stomach, vowing to the universe that if she had a daughter, she'd make her feel like they could discuss any and everything.

"I'm feeling a bit more tired than usual today, no worries." Now wasn't the time or the place. They had a room full of kids waiting on them. Maybe after they were done for the day, she'd gather the courage to let Maddi in.

They saw at least a dozen more patients, working together efficiently.

She glanced up, thinking another teen was walking in, but instead she was greeted with Jasper's smiling face. She couldn't help her reaction to seeing him, the way her nerves danced and her skin heated. She tucked her pen into the messy bun on top of her head. "Hey, what are you doing here?"

"I came with Jace and Riley to meet Linc at the batting cages. I thought I'd drive you home once you're done for the day." He was so handsome, so happy all the time. It was as if his smirk was permanently etched on his face. The only time she'd seen it slip was the night they'd found out she was pregnant.

She snuck out earlier than she needed to that morning, her fear of his regret driving her to get breakfast in town and show up an hour before the clinic opened. She thought she'd have the drive back to Jace and Axie's to figure out what she wanted to say to him.

"That's nice of you, thanks. We have three more patients to see though, do you mind waiting?"

"Not at all." Jasper tossed a baseball up into the air, catching it on the back of his hand. "I'm going to head down and hit a few balls, meet me down there when you're done?"

"Sounds good."

When he walked out of their makeshift clinic, she let out a sigh of relief. She had no clue how to untangle the mess they'd made last night. Did she regret it? Did he? She knew they needed to have an honest conversation, but she was dreading it. She'd never meant to complicate things, but when it came to Jasper, she acted out of character more than not.

She moved into the waiting area, calling the second to last patient of the day. He was blond and smiling at her in a way that she'd come to recognize as an overly confident boyhood swagger. She was surrounded every day by the absolute cockiest teens she'd ever encountered. They all strutted and flirted, winked nonstop. She'd learned to ignore them the way Maddi had done from day one.

The newest one though, the blond wannabe heartthrob, he moved in close as he made his way to the exam room. He paused, his grin turning almost wicked.

"Dude, what are you doing?" His friend stood, running his hands through his hair in apparent frustration. "She's pregnant." Callahan glanced down at her stomach, wondering if she'd popped without realizing. She frowned; no, it looked like she ate the world's largest burrito but she wouldn't think anyone would assume she was pregnant. "And can't you smell the shifter on her? She's mated."

Smell the shifter? She lifted her arm to her nose, wondering what he was talking about. She smelled like her vanilla lotion and Jasper's spicy cologne. She smelled amazing. Wait. "Did you say *mated?*" Had she stepped into an alternate universe? Maybe her blood sugar was low and she was hallucinating.

The blond one stepped impossibly closer, leaning into her neck and dragging his nose up to her ear. He was sniffing her.

Her heart started to race at the wrongness of everything that had happened or was said in the last two minutes.

Something wasn't right and nothing made any sense.

She wanted this guy away from her. Far, far away.

She felt the urge to scream, the call for help started to rise in her throat, and then, poof, he was gone.

Chapter Thirty-Four

Jasper

Jasper had some punk-ass kid pinned to the wall, growling in his face, teeth bared. He was murderous, he wanted to rip the young shifter limb from limb, ensure he would never be able to touch anyone's mate again. He could hear Callie behind him, begging him to stop, to let the boy go. She sounded scared, confused even. He couldn't though, he couldn't take a chance that this asshole would go after his mate. He'd do anything to protect her, to protect their baby. He'd kill before he let anyone hurt them.

Maddi's voice joined the frightened chorus, asking what was going on. He could hear her calling Linc on her cell, shouting for help. The kid's buddy was pleading with him, trying to explain his friend wasn't a bad guy, that he'd tried to stop him.

Jasper tightened his grip, watching as the shifter began to turn an unnatural shade of purple.

Before he could snap his neck, he was dragged away by Linc and Jace. It took both of them to pull him off the kid and out into the parking lot. He could feel himself fight them, but he couldn't seem to do anything to curb his anger.

He wasn't in control right now; his wolf was.

And if they'd learned anything about his shifter over the last couple of years, it was that he did what he wanted.

He punched Jace once, and then he was down on the ground, his hands pinned behind his back and his cheek against the hot pavement. His twin no longer acting like a concerned brother and instead taking on his pack beta persona.

"She's okay, she's safe. Callahan and the baby are safe. Maddi needs to defuse that situation and make sure that guy is okay," Linc growled, while Jasper didn't give a shit if that little prick was okay or not. "Dammit, Jasper, I don't want my mate in there by herself, do you understand? Fuck, stop fighting me."

"Riley, go in there with Maddi and help her wrap things up," Jace was barking orders with his knee in Jasper's back. "And get Callahan out here so he'll stop fighting us."

The moment Callie stepped into view Jasper stilled. He needed to make sure she was unharmed, that she was safe. He could tell she was scared and confused.

He wasn't sure she'd come to him, or let him near her. He'd showed her a part of himself she didn't know existed. Jace and Linc stepped away from him, making sure not to move any closer to Callie. To his mate. They were smart, not wanting to set him off all over again.

He stood, adjusted his clothes, and wiped his split lip. He wasn't sure which one of them had hit him, but he'd put money on it being his twin.

"Callahan, you have to go to him. He won't hurt you. I swear it." Jace had his hands on his hips, his gaze trained on her. "He's not going to calm down until he has you in his arms, and if that kid walks out here with him still pissed, it's going to get bad *fast*."

She swallowed, her hands twisting in front of her. She was hesitant, but eventually she crossed the parking lot and stepped into Jasper's embrace. He sagged instantly, the tension and anger draining out of him at her soft touch and sweet scent.

He hugged her tight, pulling her as close as he could. He let his hands roam her body, checking her for injury and replacing that young shifter's scent with his own. He nuzzled her neck, placing a soft kiss under her ear when what he really wanted to do was lick her from head to toe.

Linc let out a long, exhausted sigh. "When the fuck did this happen?" He knew Jasper's reaction to Callie was undeniable, and entirely recognizable. They were mated.

"Last night." Riley was back, which meant Maddi must be done. The teens had probably been led through the back exit so they didn't have to come near him.

"She know?" Linc, everyone, was talking like he and Callie weren't standing right next to them, listening. Jasper hugged her closer, tucking her in under his chin.

Jace glared at him. "Apparently not."

Jasper chose to ignore his brother, his pack beta. He'd had every intention of talking to Callie that morning, but she'd left as soon as the sun came up. He figured she needed a minute, needed some space. Which was why he'd come into town, had asked to drive her home.

He wasn't putting their conversation off, he simply wanted to do it right.

From the moment he'd first had her in his arms, that was all he'd ever wanted. To do right by her.

He dropped down to his knees putting his hands on her stomach, closing his eyes and listening for the baby, making sure their son okay. Jasper could hear his heartbeat, could tell he was moving around. He kissed their baby, hugging her waist.

"Do I need to call Baze?" Linc had Maddi in his arms now.

"No, we got this." Jace stepped to him, shaking his shoulder. "Come on, man, let's get you two back to the house."

***

Jasper drove Callie home, the car ride tense and silent. He hadn't been sure what to say, or how to even start the conversation. He was nervous as fuck. It was going to be hard enough to explain everything *before* he'd almost killed some cocky-ass new shifter. Once they pulled into the driveway, his cell phone rang, giving

Callie the excuse she needed to jump out of the car and head inside without him. He let her go, he knew she was safe, and she wanted space.

"Hello?"

"Hey, kid, we've got a problem." It was Maddi and she sounded uneasy.

He stiffened. "Is it that punk? He got angry parents? I'll come back to campus and apologize, explain what happened. I'm sure they'll understand." He wasn't the first shifter who lost his shit on some douche who touched his pregnant mate.

"It's not that." Maddi paused, adding to the drama of the situation. "Callahan's father was just here."

"What in the actual hell?" He let his head drop to the steering wheel, banging it around a few times for good measure. Fuck his life, for real. "He's not on his way to Jace's right now, is he?"

"No, of course not." The whole pack knew Jace took the location and privacy of his home extremely seriously. "I told him that she went on some bullshit overnight camping trip with Blake, who he assumed was my daughter by the way, and that he could meet her at my house tomorrow morning."

"Fan-fucking-tastic." He got out of his car. "I wasn't sure my evening could get any better, and wouldn't you know? It has."

"Sorry, kiddo." He could hear Maddi push her front door open, a sound he would recognize anywhere. "You want us to come over? Is there anything we can do?"

"I wish there was." He sighed. "It's time for me to be a big boy, huh?"

"You'd think that time would've already come and gone when you found out you had a baby on the way." She laughed, letting him know she was giving him a hard time. "She loves you, Jasper. She was made for you, and you were put on this earth to make her happy." She paused, the sound of Allison's giggles coming over the line. "You two are going to be just fine."

"Thanks, Maddi. Love you."

"Love you too, kiddo. Call me if you need me."

He hung up and headed into the house, stopping short when Riley and Jace were waiting for him. His twin leaned his back against the island, tossing him a beer. "You ready to tell her?"

"Nope." He twisted off the cap, downing half of it in a few long swallows.

Jace glared, his pack-beta-size irritation coming through loud and clear. "You want to try that answer again?"

"I'm not telling her tonight, bro." Jasper polished off his beer and made a gimmie motion, prompting Riley to hand him another. "She's pregnant, she's mated, and she just watched me try to murder someone for touching her, and in a surprising twist of *what the actual fuck*, her father is in town."

"Are you serious?" Riley straightened.

"Hand to god." Jasper drained his second beer.

Jace nodded, lips pursed. "What's the game plan? If that man is on his way to my house, I might go postal."

"Maddi told him she was camping with Blake. I'm taking her to meet him in the morning."

"Does she know?" Riley grabbed a beer, twisting it open and flicking the top across the kitchen into the trash.

"Not yet." He pushed away from his spot near the garage door. "I'm going to go tell her now. The rest will have to wait until after we deal with her parents." Jasper waved over his shoulder on his way out of the room; he didn't have the energy to bother to tell them good night.

The world was resting on his shoulders, threatening to crush him with every new thing that came his way.

He'd handled heavy loads, he had. He'd fought by his twin's side, he'd saved his pack, he'd killed his own father.

He'd endured beatings, he'd almost fucked up his best friend's mating.

He'd come out the other side with his humor and arrogance intact.

This though? This wasn't only about him.

This was the girl he loved. The girl he'd claimed as his own. And their baby boy.

It wasn't his present that was in danger, it was his future.

Chapter Thirty-Five

Callahan

Callahan had showered, locking the bathroom door to make sure Jasper stayed out. She had no clue what happened back at the clinic. One minute some kid was spouting the oddest stuff and the next, she thought Jasper was going to kill him. She was beyond confused. Last night Jasper had been passionate, caring, he'd been everything. This evening when he'd shown up on campus, he'd been easygoing and happy. He'd turned on a dime.

Her whole life had seemed to turn on a dime the moment she met him.

She'd never been this girl. The girl who lusted and wanted things she shouldn't have. She was lying to her parents, she was making mistakes, and complicating her life. She wasn't sure which way was up anymore. She shut off the water, drying her body with one of Jace and Axie's supple oversize towels before letting it drop to the tile floor.

She pivoted to the side, studying her body in the floor-to-ceiling mirror. She put her hand on the tiny swell of her stomach, smiling despite all the questions swimming around her skull. Their baby was growing and healthy. She couldn't help but love it.

She headed back into her room after pulling on a big t-shirt Maddi had gifted her. It was a St. Leasing baseball shirt and it had Jasper's number on the back. Maddi thought it would be a cute keepsake to have for the baby one day. It'd been so soft she hadn't been able to resist wearing it. She clicked off the bathroom light, stopping short at the sight of Jasper perched on the edge of her bed. His head was in his hands, his elbows resting on his knees.

"I know you probably don't want to see me." He glanced up, meeting her eyes and breaking her resolve a bit. He looked exhausted. "But we need to talk." He held his hands out, silently begging her to come to him.

She hesitated, like she had out in the parking lot. Her body wanted to obey, her heart too. It was her brain that made her pause. In the end, again, her brain lost. She let him guide her between his thighs, his palms rubbing along the back of her bare legs. "That was Maddi who called. Your dad is in town."

She crumpled, glad that he was there to catch her. He picked her up, settling her on his lap. "Maddi told him you were camping with Blake and you two would be back in the morning. I'm supposed to bring you to Linc and Maddi's after breakfast."

Callahan rested her head in the space between his neck and shoulder, inhaling his scent with every attempt to hold back her sobs.

The dam broke, and a flood of tears were the result.

It was too much. Last night. The altercation with the boy. Her dad being in town. She was nineteen, she was pregnant, she was scared.

She was in the arms of a man she couldn't seem to stay away from. Nothing made sense.

She let it all go, pouring her confusion and anxiety into Jasper's arms. He held her, smoothing his hand up and down her back, whispering kind words of encouragement into her ear.

He told her he'd take care of her and the baby.

He told her that everything was going to be okay, and that he'd never let anyone hurt them.

He promised her the moon, and all the stars.

Eventually, her tears exhausted her and she fell asleep in his arms.

***

Callahan woke in the middle of the night, the room pitch black, Jasper wrapped around her. He was still holding her the way he'd been when she drifted off. He hadn't left, he hadn't moved her. He was watching over her, even when she no longer needed it. She turned in his arms, careful not to disturb him. She traced his eyebrows, his cheekbones, his lips. Lips that provided the sweetest kiss and the dirtiest talk. Jasper was the whole package, and one day he would make someone incredibly happy. She'd have to watch as he finally fell in love, as he met his match.

But tonight, tonight he was hers.

Tomorrow she'd see her father, and it would go terribly, she had no doubt. She'd be hurt and he'd be angry. He'd demand she leave with him. He'd demand control of her pregnancy and the rest of her life. She choked back a fresh round of tears that threatened to fall. She would fight him, with Jasper by her side.

They were united in their decision to raise their baby, and with Jasper's strength she knew she wouldn't waver. Which meant she might very well lose her relationship with her parents.

"I can feel your worry." Jasper's hand came up, cupping her cheek, his thumb brushing against the few tears she let fall. "Please don't cry anymore, Callie baby. Everything is going to be okay." She closed her eyes, taking a deep inhale of his spicy scent. He rolled onto his back, bringing her on top of him.

His hands palmed her, kneading her flesh and moving her core against his hard length. He lifted up, capturing her mouth and kissing her until all her worries started to fade away. He expertly maneuvered them until she was sliding down his cock, gasping at how deep he was inside her. He fisted her hair, pulling her head back and arching her spine. "Do what feels good, baby."

With his help and direction, she found a rhythm, chasing a release she didn't know she needed. She let go, not caring anymore how she looked on top of him or if she woke up the entire house.

In that moment, nothing mattered except how good he felt, and how much she needed him.

"Good girl, keep going. I can feel how close you are," he growled low in his throat, something he'd done the last time they'd been together too. It was so primal and hot.

She cried out as she came, swirling her hips as he spilled inside her.

He pulled her down on top of him, hugging her close and moving her hair out of her face. "It's all going to be okay, I promise."

"One of these days, I might start holding you to all these declarations."

"Good." He kissed her forehead. "Now sleep." It was like a command and her body instantly relaxed in his hold while her eyelids grew heavy.

She drifted off to the feel of him nuzzling the side of her neck.

Chapter Thirty-Six

Jasper

They were inside a brand-new SUV with bulletproof glass and every safety feature known to man. His twin had tossed him the keys that morning on his way down the stairs to find Callie some breakfast. When he'd raised his eyebrows in question, Jace had simply shrugged and told him it was a gift for his new nephew. There was no point in arguing; his brother was protective of his pack, and that now included Callie and their baby.

"Whose car is this?" Callie rubbed her hands against the seat, peering into the back. "I haven't seen it in the garage before." She'd been driving one of Jace's extra sedans; Jasper's truck had been too large for her to navigate the mountain roads between St. Leasing and the house.

Jasper tightened his hands on the wheel, a lie poised on his tongue. At some point though, he was going to have to start telling her the truth; the deceit was piling up and starting to cripple him under its weight. "Uh, it's yours."

"What?" She huffed out a laugh. "You can't be serious."

He shrugged like an $80,000 SUV wasn't a big deal. "Jace got it for the baby. It's a gift."

"Your brother got the baby a car?" She looked around again, studying the tan interior more thoroughly. "A really nice car I could never in a million years afford? This is too much. I can't accept this."

"Nothing matters more to Jace than safety." That wasn't a lie, at all. "Certainly not money, and like I said, it was a gift. But if it makes you uncomfortable, I'll pay him for it." He reached across the console, taking her hand in his. They could argue about the outrageous gift later; they had more important issues pending. Her father. Their mating. The fact she didn't know he shifted into a damn wolf at will.

"You nervous?"

"Yes."

She squeezed his hand, and his heart soared. He was beyond thankful she was allowing him to touch her, to comfort her. He didn't know what he would've done if she'd shut him out last night.

She was his, even if she didn't understand that yet.

"He's going to be so angry with me."

"You don't have to tell him yet if you aren't ready." He took a right, pulling into campus and onto Linc and Maddi's street.

"This has been hanging over my head since we found out about the baby." She moved their joined hands to her stomach. "I don't want to spend the rest of my pregnancy dreading it." She smiled, glancing down as his thumb caressed her barely noticeable bump. "I want to enjoy this with you and your family. With the people who are happy for us, who are excited to meet this kid of ours."

He threw the car in park, putting his palm on her face, turning her to him. "I'm with you every step of the way, okay?" He waited for her to nod. "Your parents don't get a say in this. We don't need them." He kissed her sweet lips, whispering against them, "I've got you, both of you." There was so much more he wanted to tell her, but now wasn't the time.

They walked up the driveway, hand in hand. He opened the front door; he hadn't bothered knocking in a long time. This was his family, his pack, and they would always be welcome. He guided Callie inside, his hand on her lower back, trying like hell to infuse her with the strength she needed.

"Callahan." Her father rose from his seat on the couch, setting aside his cup of coffee. Jasper could feel her tense under his palm. The guy looked like Jasper assumed he would. Dark hair, graying at his temples. Ironed jeans with a crisp polo shirt. A dad bod. Sneakers. A pastor on his day off. "You stopped checking in. What's gotten into you? We were worried." He paused, his eyes moving from her to Jasper. "Who is this? Why is a boy bringing you back? Is that Blake? Have you been lying to me and your mother? What is going on here?" He took a step toward her, his arm outstretched like he was going to grab her.

Jasper's wolf reacted, it was instinctual. He put himself between them, a low growl coming out of his throat. Thankfully, Linc spoke over the potential chaos. "Jasper, why don't you come into the kitchen with me and let Callahan speak to her father."

"No."

"Now, Jasper." Baze stepped into the room, commanding him as pack alpha, leaving little room for argument. "We'll stay close, and Linc won't leave her alone."

Jasper's fingers clutched Callie's shirt. He was compelled to follow Baze's orders, but no part of him wanted to leave his mate. He'd promised her that he'd stay by her side. He whimpered, unsure which part of him would win, feeling like his heart was being torn in two.

"I'll be okay." Callie stepped around him, her hands rubbing his arms. He hesitated, ignoring Baze's low snarl at his insurrection. "I promise."

Reluctantly, he followed Baze into the kitchen, his glare never wavering from her father. Baze grabbed him by the back of the shirt, hauling him the rest of the way. "Stay right here, and *listen*. If she needs you, truly needs you, I'll let you go. I swear. I don't want to see her hurt either. She's pack."

Jasper leaned against the wall, his heart pounding. His wolf was fucking pissed and clawing to be let out. That was the last thing any of them needed, him shifting in front of Callie's father.

Linc knew things could go badly, and he'd been right to bring in Baze as backup. Jasper would've been able to go against Linc, but he'd never be able to deny his pack alpha.

He stayed silent, creeping as close to the living room as Baze would allow him, listening intently.

"Callahan, what is going on here? You stopped returning your mother's calls. I come to check on you to find you clinging to some boy? I raised you better than this. Than any of this." There was a pause. "You'll be coming home with me."

"I lied to you, and I'm so sorry." She was choking back tears. Jasper knew that sound anywhere, he'd watched her do it enough over the last couple of months. "I didn't know what else to do. I was afraid to tell you the truth."

"And what *is* the truth?"

It took several seconds for her to answer. Jasper could picture her taking a deep breath, steeling her spine and her nerves, crying anyway. "I'm pregnant."

"No."

Jasper couldn't help but snort. That had been his immediate response to the news as well.

"I'm pregnant, and Jasper brought me here to give me a safe space to decide what I wanted to do about it." She was full-on speaking through sobs now. "I knew you and Mom would be angry, that you'd force a decision on me, that you'd hide me away."

"How could you be so stupid? So reckless?" Her father paused again. "That boy, that's the father?" She must have nodded. "We're leaving. Pack your things. I'm taking you home. Your mother and I will figure out how to handle this."

"I'm not leaving. This is where I want to be."

"Yes, you are. I don't care where you want to be. You're obviously incapable of making smart choices." There was another short pause. "I'm disgusted with you. I can't even look at you. Spreading your legs for some boy who promised you the world."

There was some rustling, then Linc spoke up. "Please don't touch her like that."

Jasper's eyes flew to Baze, and the moment Baze gave him a small nod, he moved into the living room. Callie's father was dragging her down the hall; he thought that was where she was staying. Jasper's wolf took over, once again. He grabbed her father's hand and pried his fingers off her wrist. He'd been holding her so roughly, there would be bruising.

"She said she's not leaving. Respect her wishes or I will literally toss you out of this house onto your ass."

"Don't you dare speak to me that way, you arrogant son of a bitch."

Jasper glanced behind him, checking on his mate. She was sobbing, like he knew she would be. "Callie, baby, it's going to be okay."

"Like hell it will." Her father reached for her again and Jasper batted his hand away. "This punk isn't going to take care of you or that baby. He sure as hell won't marry you."

Her father was everything he assumed he'd be. Everything Callie had made him out to be. Condescending and controlling. However, the asshole had inadvertently thrown out the solution to their problem. *Marry her.* Jasper had done that the moment he'd claimed her. They were linked, together for the rest of time. They were more than married, they were mated.

Jasper pursed his lips, his gaze skirting to Linc, who simply winked, thinking the same thing he was. He knew this was bound to throw Callie for a loop, and maybe piss her off a bit. It was a necessary evil. Her father needed to leave Haxton before Jasper ended up knocking his old ass out.

"Yeah I will."

Callie and her father both said *"What?"* at the same time. Their expressions similar, their tones incredulous for different reasons.

"I want to marry your daughter." He stared her dad down. "I'm going to marry her and take care of them both. We don't need your permission or your support." He'd told Callie that from day one, and he was proving his point now.

Her father scoffed. "Don't be ridiculous."

"Dead-ass serious." Jasper positioned himself between Callie and her father, making sure he didn't attempt to grab her again. His wolf was on a hair trigger as it was.

"Get out." Callie spoke up behind him, her tone clear and harder than he'd ever heard it. "Father, get out. Go home, and I'll call you when I'm ready to talk."

She backed away, grabbing the front door and holding it open. When her dad opened his mouth, to spew some more shit he was sure, she cut him off. "I won't talk anymore about this, not today. I'm safe here, and I have to work tomorrow. I wasn't lying about the clinic. I'll call you and Mom next week." She sighed when he stayed rooted in place, his jaw on the floor. "If you don't leave, I'll let them throw you out."

Her father finally moved, slinking out of the house and tossing a death glare at Jasper on the way. She shut the door and then spun to face him, her hands on her narrow hips pulling her dress tighter and showing him that little bump he was becoming obsessed with. "You too."

"What?" He frowned, confused by her statement and that same harsh tone she'd used with her father.

"Get out, or I'll let Baze throw you out." She gestured to the door. "I don't want your damn pity proposal, and I don't want to see you right now."

"Wait, Callie. You don't understand." He took a step toward her. "It wasn't out of pity, I swear. If you'll let me explain—"

"I don't want your explanations right now, Jasper. I have fucking whiplash." He jerked back, surprised that she was cussing. "You run your one-night-only game, and then you get me pregnant. You bring me to your home to give me space, and then you sleep next to me every night. You tell me we'll co-parent as friends, and then we hook up. And now, you say you want to marry me? I don't even know which way is up anymore."

"There's so much I need to tell you, so much I want to tell you." He wasn't above pleading with her at the moment. "If you would give me a chance."

"Not today, Jasper. I need some time."

"But Callie, I'm a wolf."

Linc, who was still standing off to the side with Baze, mumbled, "For fuck's sake," and Callie blinked rapidly with a frown on her pretty face. "What?"

"I can turn into a wolf at will. I'm a shifter. I'm magic, we all are. Me and the pack. All the males anyway." He wasn't rambling in starts and stops, he was butchering his admission.

She deserved more from him, from this moment. There was no taking it back now though. He'd put it out there and he could see from the disbelief on her face that nothing he said was sinking in. He pulled his shirt off, unbuttoning and kicking off his shorts.

"Please don't shift in my living room right now." Linc shook his head as Jasper yanked off his boxers in reply. "Okay, fucking perfect. This is the exact right answer."

He ignored the sarcasm in Linc's tone. "Watch." Jasper let his wolf come to the fore, the air shimmering around him as he transformed before Callie's eyes. He kept his attention on her face, gauging her every reaction.

She gasped, her hand covering her mouth. He could hear her heart start to race. He stepped forward, resting his head against her side. Her hand was trembling, and it hesitantly rested on his fur. He pushed against her, using his weight to root her in place, to let her know this was real and he was still him. The same guy in wolf form or human.

"He's a wolf." Jasper glanced back to see both Baze and Linc nod. "And you two? Wolves as well?" They nodded again. "Make him shift back."

Baze held his stare, a deep rumble coming from his gut and commanding Jasper switch back. Within a brief moment, he stood in front of his mate with his dick in his hand. "There's so much more I need to explain to you."

"Get out." She opened the front door. "Not today."

"You can't be serious. I just told you I was fucking magic and shifted before your eyes."

She shrugged, pointing to the driveway. "Get in your kid's expensive SUV and give me some space. For some reason I can't dwell on at the moment, I don't care you're some mystical wolf creature. I care that you threw out the idea of marriage like it was an answer to a problem and not something special that should've been discussed with me first." She rested her hand on her stomach. "I'm hormonal and sad and angry, and I don't want to talk to you right now. So like I said, leave, or I'll let Baze make you."

Jasper glanced at his alpha, looking for help. Baze grabbed him gently by the shoulder. "Come on, man. Get dressed. Let's go for a drive."

He couldn't believe she was kicking him out. He couldn't believe after what he'd told her, what he'd showed her, she was still pissed as hell at him.

He had to chuckle on his way across the porch. If anything, this proved exactly what his packmates had told him. She was made for this life.

She was made to be his.

Chapter Thirty-Seven

Callahan

For the first time in her life, Callahan had been assertive. She'd kicked both Jasper and her father out of someone else's house. Ballsy, no matter which way one sliced it. She needed a minute to herself though; she needed to wrap her brain around all the insane things that had been said.

She was sitting on the back patio, a glass of green tea beside her and a giant cookie in her hand. Linc didn't make them; according to Maddi, he went to the bakery that morning to get fancy pastries for her father's visit. No amount of pretty sugar could've saved that mess though.

She took a deep breath, closing her eyes and working through the process of, well, processing. She knew her father would be angry and disappointed. She knew he'd try to throw his weight around and demand control of her life and her pregnancy. Nothing out of character had transpired there. She was prepared, from the moment she found out she was pregnant, for the conversation to go terribly.

What she hadn't counted on was Jasper saying he wanted to marry her. Then turning into a wolf the moment after she slammed the door on her father. That had been…jarring, to say the least.

The real kicker though? She didn't care he was a shifter from a long line of magical beings. No matter how hard she tried, she couldn't seem to make her brain panic about it. What pissed her off was the abrupt and ridiculous marriage proposal. She didn't want

Jasper to marry her out of obligation. She wanted her marriage to come out of love, respect, desire. Not the baby growing inside her.

"Hey, can I join you?" Maddi stepped out the back door, a chilled glass of wine in her hand. It was barely noon, but Callahan wouldn't say anything. They'd all had a hell of a morning. "How are you doing, sweetheart?"

"My father hates me, and soon my mother will too." That broke her heart more than anything. Jasper wasn't going anywhere. She knew that with every fiber of her soul. She wasn't worried about him or their relationship. They'd patch it, they'd be there for each other and the baby. Her parents though? She might never see them again. "I knew this was coming. It's my own fault really. I shouldn't have lied to them in the first place."

Maddi sat beside her, staring out at the field giving way to dense woods behind the house. "Your parents don't hate you. I can promise you that." She sighed, taking a small sip from her glass. "They're scared for you, they're disappointed in your choices. They no doubt feel out of sorts. They don't have any control over their little girl anymore, and that has to be terrifying."

"I'm scared too."

"Well, becoming a mom is scary, so your fear is justified."

She nodded. "Great. I thought maybe you'd come out here to talk me down from the ledge."

Maddi laughed lightly. "If you want someone to wax poetically about the joys of pregnancy, birth, and motherhood, then I can call Molly. She took to all of it like a woodland fairy, sprinkling goodwill and tears along the forest floor." Maddi reached out, patting Callahan's arm where it rested on the chair. "Being pregnant is exhausting and wondrous. Birth is horrifying and miraculous. Being a mom is equal parts heaven and hell. You're filled with more love than your body can contain, but if you think too hard about how much you love your children, that love turns to fear because the very thought of something bad happening to them is crippling."

"Don't sell yourself short. You're pretty poetic." Callahan shoved the rest of the cookie in her mouth, channeling Blake. "You're saying my parents will come around?"

"No."

"Did you come out here to make me feel better? I'm confused." She smiled, letting Maddi know she was kidding. She loved Maddi and was grateful for her presence in Callahan's life. Right now, she wasn't sure what she'd do without her. She'd miss her terribly once they were back in Greenly.

"You sound more like the rest of this pack every day." Maddi finished her wine. "Your parents may never get over this, sweetheart, but I promise, they don't hate you." She stood, holding her hand out to pull Callahan to her feet. "Now come on, we have plans."

"I don't want to see Jasper right now."

"Good, neither do I." Maddi winked as she led her around the side of the house to the driveway. "We're having a girls' night at Axie's." She opened the passenger door as Linc came out front and loaded Allison into her car seat. "Us and the babies. The guys are going for a run, then camping in the mountains."

Callahan watched Linc buckle his daughter in. "A run." Her eyes met his. "Every time he went for a run?"

Linc nodded, his hands on his ship. "He was taking off all his clothes and shifting into a wolf first."

"Jasper is a wolf." She closed her eyes, letting her head fall back against her seat as Linc shut the back door.

Maddi started the car, patting her arm once again. "Yes, he is. They all are. And that is why we're going to have a nice little informative girls' night with the actual expert of all things shifter."

***

Blake and Axie transformed the living room, piling the floor with pillows, blankets, and pack-and-plays for all the kiddos. There was chilled wine and sparkling water. Enough snacks to feed an entire army, and MTV's *Teen Wolf* playing on the flat-screen as a joke. Callahan was moved and grateful they'd gone through all that trouble to help cheer her up. And educate her on the family she'd be linked to through her child. She put her hand on her stomach, loving that the tiniest bump was present now.

"Pen, you're the professor, how should we start this clusterfuck of a round table?" Maddi was standing off to the side, bouncing a baby. It looked like one of the twins. Allison was sitting in Callahan's lap eating the crust off a piece of pizza.

Pen, Baze's mate, nodded. "Well, we could do a brief history lesson. That sound good?" When no one objected, she took a deep breath and began. "Shifters have been around as long as history has been recorded. The best-kept secret of our world. Men who could transform into wolves to protect their people and their land. Like most real and natural magic, it was born from the earth and the need. Native Americans—"

"*Twilight* got it right," Corey interjected, and Maddi picked up a pillow and tossed it at her head.

"Either way." Pen rolled her eyes. "Shifters lived together in villages, in tribes. The gene spreading around the earth. As time went on and the world became smaller, their secret became threatened. Humans were getting too close, questioning too much. So shifters decided the best way to avoid detection was to disperse and stop living in concentrated groups. *Packs*. As the packs thinned out to blend into the fabric of the new world, the magic within them became diluted."

Blake added, "Which is why Riley and Jasper living away from their pack puts their wolf into a hibernation. They are more human than shifter until they come home."

"There aren't many true packs left in this world. We're one of the only ones in North America." Pen cleared her throat, handing Axie Oliver's pacifier that'd fallen on the couch between them. "This pack was formed by pure accident. They didn't even know it was possible. Over time, their magic grew stronger. Baze and Jace rose as alpha and beta, the girls born from our matings have guardians, and their senses became sharper."

"Riley noticed your pregnancy days before Jasper asked you to come to dinner." Blake took Hadley from Corey and handed her a cookie. "Riley can always sense the pregnancies first, that's his superpower. He can acutely see the smallest changes in others."

"Jasper knew I was pregnant before I took that test?" Callahan was trying her best to digest all the information they were throwing her way. "That was why he invited me over?"

Blake nodded. "He wanted to be there with you when you found out. He didn't want you to go home and be scared and alone."

Jasper had been taking care of her from the moment he found out she was pregnant. It warmed her heart, and it also thawed some of her irritation toward him.

He meant what he said about being there for her and the baby no matter what.

"If this baby is a boy?"

"He'll shift, usually around puberty." Pen looked at her own son in Axie's arms. "Normal pregnancy, normal birth. Normal childhood, for the most part." She tacked on, "He would be a little stronger, more agile. No huge differences until puberty."

"Why am I not freaking out about all of this?" She shook her head, hugging Allison tighter, stealing some of her warmth. "This is life-altering news and I'm sitting here like it's nothing. This doesn't make sense."

"It will, sweetheart." Maddi laid the twin she was holding in the pack-and-play. He'd fallen asleep. "But the rest of the story isn't for us to tell."

Callahan sighed, rocking Allison side to side. *Jasper.* She missed him, but at the same time, she wasn't ready to see him. They needed to have a big talk about their future and where they went from the moment he threw out his marriage plans. "They're camping?"

Molly pointed out the back door at the mountain and the sun that was beginning to sink behind it. "If you need him, all you have to do is go outside and call him. He'll hear you."

She did need him, but she wasn't sure she was ready to hear the rest of their story.

She wasn't naïve; she could clearly see some of the things Pen and the others weren't saying out loud. Jace and Axie, Riley and Blake.

They were so young, but already living together.

Some wolves mated for life.

Was Jasper one of them?

Chapter Thirty-Eight

Jasper

Jasper was worried about Callie. He was worried she was hurting and angry. When he said he wanted to marry her, he was trying to get her father to back down. Take away his argument. He'd never wanted to upset her. He was impressed with how she'd kicked them both out of the house.

He hated that he'd been exiled to the woods though. He wanted to see her, to explain the rest of his thought process. He wanted her to know she was his and that he'd already joined their souls. No human marriage could ever compare to the connection they now shared.

"Camping is supposed to fun. You're killing our vibe." Riley kicked a booted foot out, shoving Jasper to the side. "We went on a long run, we have a fire, we have fancy-ass food thanks to your twin." He held his arms wide. "This is a great night. Act accordingly."

Jasper's need to fix things between him and his mate was all consuming. No amount of pack bonding could patch the ache in his heart. He was feeling unsettled and on edge. His wolf had enjoyed the run, of course he had. Now though, sitting here in this circle jerk was dumb. He was pacing inside him. "My wolf."

"Wants to go to his mate." Linc nodded in understanding. "After Maddi found out about us and walked away, I felt like my chest was going to crack in two. I couldn't *not* follow her. I get what you're going through."

"Great, so you won't mind if I fucking leave."

He stood, only to be jerked back down to the log he'd been sitting on by Baze. "She isn't ready to talk to you."

"No one stopped Linc from going after Maddi like a little puppy."

Baze shrugged. "I wasn't alpha then. I couldn't command him to do anything."

"Give her some time, Jasper." Keller reached over and shook his shoulder. "Try to enjoy the time with your pack while you can. Mated with a baby on the way and your sophomore year of college looming?" He laughed. "Your life will never be as carefree as it is in this moment."

***

Jasper sat up with a start, his heart pounding out a painful rhythm in his chest. He was panting, like waking from a bad dream. He glanced around, seeing the rest of his pack asleep under the stars. His wolf whimpered, urging him to move, to head down the mountain. To go to his mate.

Jasper didn't bother to tell anyone where he was going; they would know. He could feel her waiting for him, he could feel her patience. She wasn't hurt; the baby was okay. She was ready to talk, so she'd called to him.

He took his time, staying in human form for the descent. He needed the extra time to organize his thoughts. He didn't want another stupidly blurted marriage declaration to mess things up worse.

When he entered through the back gate, he found Callie sitting on the patio, one of his sweatshirts wrapped around her shoulders. She smiled, glancing behind her at the pile of bodies in the living room. "I don't want to wake them."

He nodded, coming to sit beside her. "I didn't want to wake the guys either."

"Molly said you would hear me when I called you."

He smiled, his lips against her shoulder. "Molly believes in all the best parts of our magic, of the bond between mates."

"Is that what we are? Mates?"

He sighed, moving to kneel before her. "I wanted you from the first moment you blew me off. I can see now it was my wolf, excited for the chase. When you agreed to give me one night, I couldn't get enough of you. I couldn't bring myself to leave your body. I couldn't bring myself to send you home. I watched you as you slept, more than once."

She narrowed her pretty eyes. "This all sounds very suspect. You know that, right?"

"Oh, I'm aware. Me, my wolf, we've become rather obsessed with you." He smiled, trying to reassure her everything was all right. "When Riley told me you were pregnant, I had a mini freak-out moment. But then it was like this new sense of purpose came over me. Once you knew too, my wolf was all smug and proud of himself. He wanted to take care of you, both of you."

"That's why you were so good to me that night? Your wolf demanded it?"

He pursed his lips, contemplating her question. "Yes and no. He and I wanted the same thing. We were harmonious, which, I think, helped keep me so calm." He reached for her hands. "I didn't know you were meant to be mine. I knew I cared for you, and I loved our baby, but after we were together the other night..." He wasn't sure how to word the rest, the biggest truth that needed to be spoken between them. "Wolves mate for life, Callie."

She was quiet for a few moments, as if she was absorbing the reality of their situation. "The baby, was that what bonded us? Have we been mated this whole time?"

He shook his head, bringing their joined hands up to kiss the back of hers. "It was the other night. When we were together. I swear I didn't do it on purpose. I didn't know. When I didn't use a condom, there was nothing between us and that sealed your fate. I claimed you that night."

"Are you telling me you accidentally claimed me during a pity fuck?"

"Did you just say pity fuck?" He couldn't help but chuckle as he moved forward and settled between her thighs. "Nothing about that night had anything to do with pity, baby. I wanted you so very much. And yeah, I didn't intend to claim you, but fate doesn't make mistakes. To be fair, I did ask you to stop me and you kept begging for more."

She rolled her pretty eyes. "When you told my father you planned on marrying me?"

He kissed her lips, stealing a moment to show her how much he craved her, grateful she was letting him touch her. "It was the easiest way I could think of to get him to leave you alone, to give him what he wanted. I was barely able to contain my wolf as it was; if he'd grabbed you one more time, we would've had a huge problem. Even though I hadn't gotten a chance to tell you everything, I knew we were already more than married. Our souls are tied together, bound for eternity." He kissed her again, pushing her back on the lounger where she was perched. "I was put on this earth to make you happy, to love you. In that one instant, you became my entire universe."

"Pretty words for a self-proclaimed fuck-boy, don't you think?"

He couldn't help but laugh again. "You've got a dirty mouth tonight." He stood, removing his pants before bending down to pull off her pajama shorts as well. "I like it." He spread her thighs, moving in to lick at her core. "I'm a one-woman fuck-boy from now on." He nipped and sucked his way to her mouth, kissing her as he sunk his cock inside her warmth.

Her gaze flew to the glass patio doors. "Who closed the curtains?"

He sucked on her neck, letting her flesh go with a pop and marking her because his wolf wanted to. "Axie. She flipped me the bird and a wink while she did it."

Callie put her hands over her face, speaking behind her fingers. "They know we're out here naked?"

"Baby, when it comes to mated couples, always assume someone's naked. Always close the curtains, always knock three times." He began to move, thrusting into her carefully so he didn't throw them off the damn chair. He pulled her hands away from her face so he could continue to kiss her as he fucked her senseless in his brother's backyard.

He was so damn happy to be inside her perfect body. Everything felt right in his world now that she was back in his arms.

She knew the truth and she was still here, letting him love her the way his wolf demanded.

She would have questions. There was more they would need to figure out. For now though, this was what they both needed. To erase the distance between them.

Chapter Thirty-Nine

Callahan

The guys had come down the mountain, claiming they smelled the bacon cooking in Jace's kitchen. Jasper still got his night under the stars. He and Callahan slept tangled together on a blanket in the grass. She'd be lying if she said her back wasn't killing her, but it'd been worth it. Jasper had been sweet, romantic, all the things he'd swore he could never be. Hearts and flowers, over and over.

The whole pack was scattered around the kitchen and spilling into the living room, plates balanced on laps and babies crawling all over the place. Jasper was feeding Allison while Callahan was holding one of Molly's twins. She could never tell them apart. She wasn't sure if she was holding Bhodi or Riot.

One thing she knew for sure: she was happy and at peace.

Her world suddenly made so much sense.

"When are you two headed back to Greenly?" Keller had the other twin in his arms. "Fall semester starts before too long, right?"

"Few weeks." Jasper glanced across the kitchen to his brother. "I'm sure Jace is counting down the days."

Jace's smile was wicked. "Twenty days."

"Two shifters, one Barbie doll, and one baby momma." Riley laughed. "Our house is getting crowded."

"Jasper and Callahan are moving into the house across the street." Jace took a prim bite of his omelet.

"I didn't know it was for sale." Blake shoved a cinnamon roll in her mouth.

Jace grinned. "It wasn't."

"You bought us a house?" The car, the house, it was all too much and more than she was used to. Jasper wasn't controlling like his twin. He cared about her safety, it mattered to him if she ate and got enough sleep. He didn't make big decisions without speaking to her first. Well, other than bonding them for eternity.

"*I* bought us a house." Jasper wrapped his arms around her waist, his palms resting on their baby. "And I paid Jace back for the SUV. I take care of you. That's the way this works."

"Well, except for the nannies I'm vetting, and doctors I'm doing background checks on." Jace shrugged. "You'll need an OBGYN in Greenly."

Callahan didn't bother to argue; she didn't even want to. She was having a hard time distinguishing which reactions were because she was now considered pack, and which ones were because she trusted Jace. In the end, it was all to keep the baby safe, so it was okay in her book.

"Do we get to submit baby names?" Axie was perched on the island, Jace leaning between her thighs. "I have a list started in my phone."

"Same." Riley raised his fork in the air.

Callie glanced at Jasper, her eyes narrowed. "Riley knows what I'm having, doesn't he?" It made sense; if he could sense a pregnancy at fetal pole stage, then he should be able to sense the gender.

"Uh, well—"

"He knows." Jasper cut off a blushing and stammering Riley.

Her gaze traveled around the kitchen, taking in how many pack members were looking anywhere but at her. "How many of you know? Raise your hands."

Every hand raised. She scoffed. "Nice. Okay, tell me. Boy or girl?" She turned in her mate's arms, her eyebrows raised in question. "Well?"

He grinned down at her, holding her close enough that her bump pressed against his hips. He kissed the side of her neck, whispering against her skin. "It's a boy."

She gasped, unable to help her initial reaction. "A shifter." She was still learning, still digesting everything it meant to be in a pack, to know the people she cared for turned into wolves and ran around the woods at night for fun. "Okay. Is there anything else I should know? Now's the time, right?"

"Nope." Jasper rocked her side to side, playfully. "We're having a boy. He'll be a shifter like his dad. We're mated. That's it."

"Is it?" Axie gestured with her head toward Riley and Blake. "I thought there was one more piece of your past you needed to explain."

Blake pouted out her bottom lip. "Ouch, lover. Whose side are you on?"

"It's better it comes out now. You know I'm right." Axie wrapped her arm around Blake, smacking a kiss on her cheek.

Riley's arms were crossed over his chest and Linc looked downright giddy.

Callahan was completely lost and becoming more nervous by the second. "Can someone tell me what's going on? I'm kind of freaking out here."

"I'm going to explain everything, I promise." Jasper picked her up, carting her out of the kitchen and toward the stairs. "I feel like this conversation would go better if I could mumble the truth against your pussy as I provide you with multiple orgasms."

***

Jasper

The pack continued to eat their breakfast as Jasper and Callahan went upstairs. And he told her. Everything about that night with Riley and Blake. Once he dropped the Blake bomb? She'd gone nuclear. "Is it the threesomes you have issue with, or the fact that Blake was part of my last one?"

Callahan's arms were crossed over her ever-growing breasts, pushing them up and making his mouth water. "Honestly? I'm not sure."

He nodded, edging closer to her, cautiously. "Is it jealousy? Or is it pregnancy hormones?"

Her eyes narrowed. "If you think blaming my reaction to you doing anal with one of my friends on our son..."

"You're right, I'm an idiot." He knelt before her. "But I'm an idiot who is so completely in love with you, I've already forgotten every other girl I've ever met." It was a sappy sentiment, but the truth. Callie was the only woman in the world who mattered. Hell, who existed. Riley would never hear another threesome joke come out of his mouth. "Also, baby, did you say anal? Those lips of yours are getting dirtier by the day."

"You're a mess."

"So I've been told." He reached up, cupping her face with his hands. "So, like, you ready to try anal or...?"

"You're a mess, and you're not as cute as you think you are."

"Riley and I were dumb kids, saddled with a future we knew would be absolute. We sowed our wild oats, hard. There's no denying that." He sighed, silently praying his son was a better teenager than he'd been. Well. Actually, he was. Jasper was only nineteen. "What happened with Blake—"

"I get it. I don't know how, but I do." Callahan smiled, resting her forehead against his. "Thank you for telling me after Axie forced you to."

"I was always going to tell you." He pushed her knees apart, dragging her panties from under her sundress.

He kissed her lips, using his body to lay her flat on the bed before hooking her thighs around his shoulders. "See? Now could you think of a better way to have that conversation?" He licked her center, loving that she was already dripping for him. Her fingers threaded into his hair, her hips begging for more.

He slid two fingers inside her pussy, humming in appreciation when she moaned his name like a plea. "You are everything." He nibbled on her inner thigh. "You own me." He used his tongue along with his fingers, working her as close to the edge as he could. "My heart." She growled when he stopped just short of her first orgasm, moving up her body and tugging down his shorts. He surged inside her. "My soul."

His wolf took over, wanting to claim her over and over again, every damn day until the end of time.

***

Jace, downstairs with the pack

Jasper did a lot of groveling, and after a few minutes Callie let out a few giggles.

After that, the noises turned pretty incoherent.

Jace didn't care. He was still pissed.

"I demand I get my house back immediately."

Chapter Forty

Seven Months Later

Jasper

Jasper loved his twin, his pack, and his mate. But nothing compared to the love he felt the first time he held his son. West Sumner Franklin. West was Maddi's maiden name and Sumner was Linc's last name. He had red hair and pale skin. He was his mother's spitting image, and when they went out as a group, people assumed Riley was his father. Jasper didn't mind.

"Babe, can you bring me some water?" Callie was breastfeeding and always thirsty. If he thought he'd been obsessed with her pregnant breasts, they didn't hold a candle to the ones he had to share with his son.

He walked into the nursery, taking in his beautiful mate in the soft glow of the lamplight. It was the early in the morning, and the sun was rising in the sky. Their baby was cradled in Callie's arms, his tiny head the only part of him visible. He loved to snuggle into his mother while she fed him. The surest way to piss off their son was to have him get cold.

"Have I told you today how beautiful you are?"

She laughed softly, careful not to startle the baby. "It's seven am, so no, not yet." She smiled up at him as he sat her water on the side table and dipped to kiss her lips.

He sat on the floor, his back against the crib. The room was a gift from Maddi and Linc. They said since Jace helped make the house available and picked out Callie's car, they wanted to do the only thing left. The space was calming, lots of muted colors and soft textiles. He was sitting on a rug so plush, it could double as a mattress.

West was born the seventh of January, meaning Callie finished her finals almost nine months pregnant and completely exhausted.

She was so tiny, her massive belly made walking around campus from class to class a chore. Jasper, Riley, and Blake helped as much as they could. But Callie was adamant no missed lectures for her.

Today was the first day Jasper wouldn't be with them. Classes started back up. Even though Jace had vetted Colorado's best nannies, Callie decided to take the semester off. She'd go back in the fall, once the baby was older and she was feeling steadier on her feet as a new mother.

Jasper supported her decision. He'd done so in the beginning, there was no reason to stop now. His mate was brilliant. One semester behind wouldn't hold her back. She wanted to go into nursing, having enjoyed working with Maddi at the clinic so much.

"What time will your parents be here?" Jasper checked his watch. His first class wasn't until nine.

Callie leaned back, her eyes closed. "Soon. They left around six to make it here before you had to leave." She was tired. Always so tired. He helped as much as he could, giving West bottles with milk she'd pumped. He was still so young, only a few weeks old.

Jasper couldn't wait for the day that he was more, uh, durable. He wanted to run and play and hear him giggle and call his name. He was trying to *enjoy every stage*, advice from Molly, but his kid felt breakable, and that was terrifying.

"It's sweet they wanted to come early to see me." He winked when she picked her head up, her sleepy gaze meeting his.

Callahan's parents had come around near the end of her pregnancy. They'd met for dinner, and then they came for a visit. It was a slow recovery process, but they were obsessed with their grandson. They'd come to the hospital the day after he was born, and they were coming to stay with them for a week to help Callie adjust to not having Jasper at home all day.

The pack had come to visit too, although not all at once. They wouldn't've been able to fit in their small two-bedroom home, and all of them at the same time was too much for Callie right now.

Jace had been right. The house was a good investment. Once they were done with it, it'd be easy enough to rent to some college kids. They'd stay in Greenly only long enough for both of them to graduate.

When they'd left Haxton and his family, Callie sobbed the whole three-hour car ride back. She told him that was where she was supposed to be, the only place she'd ever felt at home, at peace.

He'd move anywhere for her. There wasn't anything he wouldn't do to make her happy.

If that meant posting up beside his surly brother and living in the mountains for the rest of his life, he'd do it. When Callie had decided on a degree path, so had he. He wanted to coach. He wanted to mentor the next round of young shifters, give them a safe space the way his coaches had given him, his twin, and his best friend.

He wasn't sure if he liked his family that much, or if it was the underlying pull of the pack. Either way, he was content with the idea of moving back to a small town to raise his son.

"Hey, little family." Blake tiptoed into the room, and her face lit up at the sight of her nephew. "I missed him. I used my key."

Jasper rolled his eyes. "Once the doc clears my girl for more than kisses, you'll need to start knocking."

Callie finished feeding the baby, then passed him to Blake. She and Riley were over pretty much every day. Jasper didn't mind, and as long as Callie didn't either, they could come and go as they pleased. It was nice to have the extra hands, and it helped him and Callie get a couple hours of alone time each day.

"I'm done with classes around three," Blake said. "After your parents leave next week, I can come by on my way home to take a feeding or whatever you need."

His mate curled up in the glider. "Packs are the way to go. I don't know how people survive without one."

He stood, scooping her into his arms. "Good thing you'll never have to find out." Blake took her place, rocking West back to sleep and singing him a lullaby completely off key. "I'm taking her back to bed for an hour, you good?"

"I'm good until Riley finishes making us all breakfast and comes to steal him."

Jasper laid his mate in their bed, chuckling when he saw she was already asleep.

He climbed in next to her, pulling her into his arms.

He took a deep breath, completely in love and at peace with the way his life had turned out.

***

And the pack kept growing...

"You two are beyond annoying." Wren turned her back on the twins, Bhodi and Riot. Giving attention to their antics only tended to escalate the situation. "If Uncle Keller finds out about this, you'll be grounded for a month." She sipped the mixed drink Oliver handed her when she reached the top of their mountain. Her father, Jace, owned it, but it belonged to all of them, to their pack.

She'd been raised at the base of it, staring up at its peak from her bedroom window. She'd been raised with the kids around her too. The last sixteen years of her life she'd spent in the middle of overprotective wolves and the mates who loved them.

Haxton, Colorado was a sanctuary for her family, and life beyond its borders was as terrifying to her as it was alluring.

"What Dad doesn't know won't hurt him." Bhodi rolled his glacier blue eyes. "So don't be a snitch." He tossed a rope up to his brother Riot, missing the connection the first time, but got it the second.

Their names needed to be reversed. Aunt Molly said she should've taken a few weeks to get to know them before she assigned the monikers. Riot was peaceful and easygoing, where Bhodi was loud and in constant motion.

Wren scrunched up her nose. "Have I ever told on you before? Why would I start now?"

She stalked farther into the clearing, joining the rest of her family where they lounged around their campsite.

They'd been coming into the mountains on their last weekend of summer freedom for as long as she could remember. As the kids got older, the parents agreed to stay home.

Hadley had turned twenty that summer, and tomorrow she'd head back to college in Denver, taking Allison with her. Those two had been best friends since birth.

Oliver, Uncle Baze and Aunt Pen's son, had been Wren's neighbor her entire life. This would be her first year without him. He was officially a college freshman, leaving in a matter of days. Wren wouldn't be alone though: Riot and Bhodi were seniors at St. Leasing, West a junior, Cooper and Chloe freshmen. They were all spaced out more or less a year apart.

"Those two going to survive whatever they're planning, or do I need to step in?" Oliver held his arm out, tucking her into his side. They were close. Not brother and sister, more like best friends. Objectively she knew he was gorgeous, so gorgeous she certainly couldn't look at him like a sibling. He had dark hair like his dad, and he was broody like Uncle Baze. Brilliant like Aunt Pen, though.

She twisted her lips, staring up at the mountain peak. "Not sure to be honest."

West laughed, waving away their concern. "They'll be fine. They always are."

"Not true. Remember when Bhodi broke his femur rappelling down the stone turret on campus?" Cooper had blond curls like his mother, blue eyes to match as well. He was helping West as they got tents set up for everyone. They'd drawn the short straws that year. "He was in that cast for weeks."

Weeks, instead of months. He was a shifter, after all.

"Aunt Molly was so worried until she found out it was nothing more than a dare. Remember that?" Chloe, Cooper's twin, who mirrored their fiery-haired father. "She made the doctor wrap his cast in bright pink. Then she drew hearts and flowers all over it."

"He used it to his advantage though." Allison giggled, turning to watch both boys as they worked together. "He told all the girls at public school parties that he chose pink for his little cousin and then let her draw all over it."

Chloe snorted. "When in truth, he wouldn't let me near it with a pen because he said I'd mess up the aesthetic."

Wren sipped her drink and watched as the people she loved laughed and talked, sharing memories of days gone by. She knew a lot of kids would feel trapped inside the boundaries of a small town and the mountains that formed it.

Not her.

She felt safe and protected.

She wasn't naïve, and her father had never tried to hide who he was and what he did. He was a powerful man, respected and feared.

To her though, he was simply *Dad*. He tucked her in at night, he came to her dance recitals, he brought her flowers on Valentine's Day, and checked her closet for monsters every night for a solid month after West convinced her to sneak into a scary movie.

She was happy where she was.

Her family, though, they were slowly leaving, one by one.

First Hadley, then Allison, now Oliver.

Riot and Bhodi would be next. She had one year left with them.

She wasn't sure what she would do when it was her turn. She couldn't imagine a life outside of Haxton, Colorado.

"I'll miss this." Oliver sighed against her side, drawing her attention back to the now. "This mountain, these nights under the stars. You."

His words made her heart soar and ache at the same time. "I'll miss you too." She turned to face him, draping her legs over his thighs. "You'll come home though, right? For breaks and the holidays? And then you'll be back next summer."

He shrugged. "I guess so." He gestured to Hadley and Allie where they sat across the fire huddled together and laughing at some story West was telling. "They seem removed though, don't they? More distant with every year that passes. Their life isn't here anymore, only their family."

"Okay, you guys ready?" Riot came into the clearing, clapping his hands together.

They all stopped, turning to the barest face of their mountain. They'd been talking about doing this for years, but hadn't figured out how to accomplish it until Bhodi and Riot got old enough to put their wicked minds together. Riot had a rope wrapped around his waist and gloves on his hands as he lowered his twin carefully down from the peak.

They watched as Bhodi hung, suspended in the air, a can of black spray paint in his hands. When he was finished, his brother lowered him to the ground and they stood in a line, admiring his work. "I don't think I did half bad."

"I agree. Good job, bro." Riot and Bhodi high-fived, congratulating each other.

"What do you think, Wren? Your dad going to be beyond pissed?"

Oliver wrapped his arm around her shoulders while West took her hand. The connections continued down the line. Arms linking, and bodies snuggled together until they stood in a united, unified line.

"Probably." She couldn't help but smile, her eyes getting a little misty.

Claimed in large black letters on their mountain for the world to see.

It belonged to them, and them to each other.

"It's perfect."

<u>PLAYLIST</u>

I love College by Asher Roth

Night Changes by One Direction

Don't Blame Me by Taylor Swift

I'm Not In Love by Ber

Nothing's All The Time by Ashley Kutcher

Flight Risk by Tommy Lefroy

Dirty Thoughts by Chloe Adams

Plot Line by Emlyn

Upside Down by Mothica

Maybe, I by Dec Rocs

Keep It To Myself by Ellise

Okay by Chase Atlantic

Chance with You by Sky on Fire

Baby by Elvis Drew

Pub Feed by The Chats

Bad Kids by TTRRUUCES

ABOUT THE AUTHOR

L.P. lives in Austin, Texas with her husband, two daughters, two dogs, and a plant-killing cat.

Writer, business owner, and office manager, L.P. says she loves to read as much as she loves to write. Reading a good book is her reward after writing one. In her spare time—ha!—she fosters puppies for a rescue organization based in Austin.

Connect with L.P.:
Website: www.lpmaxa.com
IG: @lpmaxa_author
TikTok: @lpmaxa_author
Twitter: @lpmaxa
FB: pages/LP-Maxa/1442560722667127

www.BOROUGHSPUBLISHINGGROUP.com

If you enjoyed this book, please write a review. Our authors appreciate the feedback, and it helps future readers find books they love. We welcome your comments and invite you to send them to info@boroughspublishinggroup.com.

Follow us on TikTok and Instagram, and be sure to sign up for our newsletter for surprises and new releases from your favorite authors. Are you an aspiring writer? Check out www.boroughspublishinggroup.com/submit and see if we can help you make your dreams come true.

Love podcasts? Enjoy ours at www.boroughspublishinggroup.com/podcast.